MIDWAY

THE HARVESTING SERIES BOOK 2

MELANIE KARSAK

CLOCKPUNK PRESS

Midway
Clockpunk Press, 2014

Published by Clockpunk Press
Editing by Becky Stephens Editing
Proofreading by Rare Bird Editing
Cover art by Deranged Doctor Design

❀ Created with Vellum

For Dad

MELANIE KARSAK

CHAPTER ONE

"TILT-A-WHIRL, tilt-a-whirl, tilt-a-whirl! Come on ride my tilt-a-whirl! I'll whirl you round the world," I barked to the mostly empty aisles at the Allegheny Fairgrounds.

I looked up and down the aisles. The place was like a ghost town. While bags of pink and blue cotton candy hung in the food joints, cherry red candy apples glistened in the sunlight, and over-grown stuffed purple monkeys hung at the game booths, ripe for winning, no one was around to stuff themselves with carnie delights. The smell of kettle corn still perfumed the air, but for a carnival that was usually packed with excited townies, I swore I wouldn't be surprised if a tumbleweed blew down the row.

After a bit, two young boys came up to my line. They were the only kids around. The older looked to be about twelve. The younger, a good two inches under my height bar, had pulled himself up to full height and tried not to meet my eyes.

"Tickets," I said to them.

Confidently, the older boy handed me his ticket and passed through. The younger boy hesitated. Guessing he'd be all right, I let him through. The older boy slapped him a high five when they thought they were out of earshot.

I turned the key and started the ride. The boys smiled at me. I waved to them.

"Hey Cricket," Harv, the balloon-pop agent across the aisle, called to me. "Where is everyone? Allegheny Fairgrounds is usually packed. I'm gonna go hungry."

I leaned over the gate and twirled my blonde braid, checking out the split ends. "I heard someone say it's the flu keepin' people home. You know they closed LAX? I hear it's gettin' real serious. You get a flu shot?"

"Naa. Damned thing always gives me the flu. You know, Bud's got it. He's been laid up in his RV all day."

"Anyone been by to see him?"

Harv shrugged. "He's grouchy when he feels good. I don't imagine he'd be a barrel of laughs when he's sick."

"No man is. Even the common cold has you all actin' like a bunch of babies."

"This coming from a blonde," Harv replied with a laugh.

"You better watch yourself. I'll come pop your balloons."

"Baby, a grenade couldn't pop those balloons," he said with a laugh.

I turned back to the boys. They were all smiles; round and round they spun. Since no one else was around, I let it run until they signaled they'd had enough.

Around nine o'clock that night, the owner, Mr. Marx,

came by. I had not seen a soul on the fairway since the boys left. "Sorry, Cricket. We're going to teardown to get ready for the jump to Cincinnati. We're just burning juice and not making a dime. This place is dead; not a soul here."

"All right then," I replied, and Mr. Marx wandered off. I realized he hadn't said a word about when he would pay us for Allegheny Fairgrounds, dead or not.

Moments after he left, the first of the evening fireworks shot across the sky. The dark sky was illuminated with gold and pink. I waited for a moment, expecting to hear the excited *oohs* and *ahhs* that usually followed what was a pretty measly fireworks display, but there was nothing, just the pop and crackle of the fireworks, followed by silence. Eerie.

I whistled for Puck, my mangy mixed breed and the only male I swore I would ever truly love. After a few minutes, the hound-shepherd mix with honey-colored eyes appeared looking dirty and happy. I found him about a year ago. Well, actually, he'd found me. We were getting ready to leave Crawford County Fairgrounds when he showed up at the tilt begging for scraps. I made the mistake of feeding him a leftover funnel cake, and after that, I couldn't shake him. He was a mischievous little devil, and Vella, the tarot reader, gave me the idea for his name: Puck. She said it was the name of a rascally faerie creature. It fit him. From that moment on, Puck and I were always together. More than once, a growl and flash of teeth from Puck had gotten me out of a jam. I loved that mangy mutt.

"Up to no good, were ya?" I asked, scratching him on the head. He licked my hand and wagged his tail. I closed up my till and headed to the bunk house to look for some extra muscle to help with the teardown. As I passed through the midway I saw most of the other joints and booths were already closed. Mama Rosie was just closing up the snake show when I came by.

"Marx closed down everyone up here already?" I asked her.

"They're all sick, Sug," she replied as she dropped one of her small snakes into her bra. I shivered. Everyone loved Mama Rosie, but no one understood her relationship with her *babies*. She always had one hanging out of her bra, hanging around her neck, or stuffed in her clothes. Mama was a big woman who liked to wear baggy, loud-colored gowns. I hated sitting next to her at dinner. You never knew when one of the *babies* might suddenly slither out of her hibiscus-print dress.

I set my box down and helped her push the trailer door closed. "How about you, Mama? You feelin' all right?"

"I think I ate something bad at lunch, but I'll be fine. You headed back to the bunks?"

"I guess. I was hopin' Beau and the boys would come give me a hand."

"Sug, Beau would give you a hand, arm, leg, or toe if you asked. Why don't you give that boy a chance?"

"Oh, Mama Rosie, I don't feel nothin' like that for him."

"But you run off with townies often enough."

"Well, we all have needs."

Mama Rosie laughed loud. "You got that right. I thought maybe you were hoping someone would marry you out of the life."

"And give up all this?"

Mama Rosie hooted again, her boisterous laughter filling the empty aisles.

While the smell of Chinese food, funnel cakes, and fried sausage still filled the air, there was no one around. Power was still on, so the midway sparkled in a rainbow of light, but the place was like a ghost town. I had never seen it like that, and since I'd practically grown up in the carnival, that was saying something. Several game booth agents had even left their plush hanging—now that was odd.

As Mama and I passed by Iago's Traveling Torture show, Mr. Iago came out. I winced. After three years of traveling with Great Explorations carnival, I had yet to warm up to Mr. Iago. His show was creepy. I'd once had a look inside. The place was hung with all kinds of pictures of people being tortured, and he had old torture devices like the rack, an iron maiden, a wheel of fortune, and other small harmful contraptions. Mr. Iago was as creepy as his show. On the outside he looked normal enough, just a funny-looking little bald man with too-big-ears and a pointed nose, but it was what I felt coming from inside him that set me on edge. I never looked him in the eye.

"Mama Rosie, Cricket," he called politely.

"You headed back too, Mr. Iago?" Mama called cheerfully.

"Yes, ma'am, I am," he replied softly.

"You make any scratch today?" Mama asked him.

"Well, I don't like to discuss finances," he told her in his quiet manner.

"He don't like to discuss finances," Mama said mockingly to me. "All right, Mr. Iago. You just go on with yourself then."

"No offense, Mama Rosie," he replied quietly.

"Of course not," she said and rolled her eyes at me.

When we got back to the bunk houses there were half a dozen people sitting outside at a picnic table listening to the radio. I spotted Mr. and Mrs. Chapman. They owned three of the grab joints; Mrs. Chapman waved to us. She was a biblical woman whose savory corndog breading had won top prize at a competition last year. If you didn't mind hearing her recite verse all day, she was fine to be around. Red and Neil, two ride jockeys, were there as well. Red ran Big Eli; Neil ran the swings. The resident lot lizard, Cici, was snuggled up to Red. I was surprised to see Vella there as well. Vella, the tarot reader, was a Romanian immigrant who called herself the only authentic Roma, which she said meant gypsy, in America. Even though she was just a little older than me, Vella scared me. She'd never done anything to me and was really nice, but she scared me all the same. The others said she was dead-on accurate with her readings and often had bad news to give. I didn't want to be around anything like that.

"What's the news?" Mama Rosie asked.

"Lord, help us! This flu is something else. They have quarantined almost every city on the west coast: LA, Seattle, Portland, San Francisco. . .you name it. They got the national guard on the highways keeping people out," Mrs. Chapman said.

She was quiet then. We listened: "And inside Portland Central Hospital, military personnel have opened fire on seemingly-rabid patients," a female reporter was saying. "Reports from the scene indicate that a riot broke out at the hospital when patients, suffering from side-effects of what now seems to be a pandemic flu, began attacking other hospital patients and employees. CDC officials have confirmed that increased violence appears to be associated with the afflicted and continue to advise everyone to avoid direct physical contact with those with the illness. Martial law has been instituted in all major west coast cities and cities across the south. Cities across the north-east and central US have issued a curfew. There have been reports of runs on banks, grocery stores, and fueling stations."

"What are they sayin' on TV?" I asked.

Red shook his head. "We can't get a signal in. No one's dishes are working."

"President was on the radio. Told everyone to be calm," Cici said.

"Easy for him to say. They probably got him stashed in a bunker somewhere," Mr. Chapman replied.

"Highways are gonna be backed up. And nobody's gonna be interested in a fair, not at Allegheny and not in Cincinnati. But I bet if we don't jump, Marx is gonna stiff us," I told the others.

They nodded.

"Well, if y'all will give me a hand, I'll pay back the favor," I told Red and Neil.

"No problem, Cricket. You see Beau around?"

I shook my head. "I just came lookin' for him."

"He's sick," Vella said. She rarely spoke, so when she

did, we all turned to her. "Leave him be," she added, her voice still thick with her Romanian accent.

Vella had been shuffling her cards the whole time we'd been listening to the radio. Apparently I wasn't the only one who noticed.

"What do the cards say about this flu, Vella? Should we hit the road? Stay put?" Mama Rosie asked.

"Devil's work," Mrs. Chapman whispered under her breath.

"They say the same thing over and over again: the Tower." She laid out a card for us to see.

When Mr. Iago leaned in to look, I moved away. My skin crawled having him so close. I took a step toward the other end of the table and put my hand on Mrs. Chapman's shoulder. She patted my fingers. On the card Vella had laid out was the image of a tower on fire, two naked people falling from it to the ground.

"What does it mean?" Mama Rosie asked.

"The end of a way of life. Chaos will pave the way in a new world for those who can survive the destruction."

"That's cheerful," Red said.

Vella picked the card back up. She looked up at me. "Can you let me know when you're going to head out? I'd like to caravan."

I smiled and nodded. I wasn't really interested in her gloom and doom, but I sure didn't want to be on the road alone in a time like this.

Red, Neil, and I headed back to the rides and started the breakdown process. It wasn't easy with just the three of us, but Neil was good with the lift, and I had the breakdown

down-pat. We had the tilt loaded onto the flatbed in no time.

"I've never seen a girl as good with a wrench as you are, Cricket," Red told me as we headed over to the swings.

"Don't hurt none that my daddy put one in my hand about a minute after I was born," I replied with a laugh.

"I met your daddy back in the 80s. We worked Maverick Carnival together for about a year."

"For real? I didn't know that."

"Boy, your daddy, there wasn't a mark he couldn't clean out or a townie whose eye he couldn't catch. I think your daddy was born for the carnie life."

"He loved it. That's the truth," I replied. I loved talking about my daddy. Since he'd died three years ago, I felt so lonely for him. Anytime someone had a story to share about him I was all ears.

Daddy had just finally saved and borrowed enough to buy a used tilt-a-whirl when he started looking a little red in the cheeks from time to time. My daddy had always been a ride jockey, but now he would be a ride owner, and a "tilt man," a title that made him proud. He liked the idea of tweaking the ride, playing with the gears and brakes. It was a dream for him. Not a month after getting the ride, however, I found him lying dead of a heart attack. He'd been working on one of the cars. Doctor said a life full of eating nothing but carnival food will do that to you. I'd thought about leaving the carnival, but after my daddy had worked so hard, I couldn't. I became a tilt girl. The ride was like his living memorial. Every time a child smiled or laughed on that ride, I knew my daddy was smiling in heaven.

"I never did meet your mama," Red told me then turned to Neil. "You ever meet her?"

Neil shook his head. "Someone said you look like her, Crick."

"Yeah, I suppose so. I probably wouldn't know her anymore. Last time I talked to her she said she'd dyed her hair red," I replied. My mom and dad had split when I was young. She had married and started a new life. We rarely talked. She was like a stranger to me. I didn't think on her much.

We worked on the swings. They were an easy break down, and we were done and packed in less than two hours. The Big Eli, as we called the Ferris Wheel, was another story altogether, and it was already after one in the morning.

"Let's get it first thing tomorrow," Red said. "I'm feeling my bones."

Relieved, I nodded. I didn't want the boys to know, but every muscle in my body was aching, and Puck had started whining for his dinner an hour before. I wasn't going to argue. "Just knock in the mornin'," I called to Red. "I'm over by the creek at the edge of the west parking lot. Wasn't room left in the back when I got here," I added.

"Well, that will teach you not to play around in town next jump," Red replied with a laugh, and we went our separate ways, Neil and Red chatting as they went the other direction.

Back in the parking lot, I crawled into the cab of my

truck, my home away from home. When I was a game agent, I used to drive a small RV, but I needed a semi to haul the tilt so I gave up my RV, managed to get a CDL license, and now lived in the cab of my truck. It wasn't too bad, and if it started to feel real tight, I would stay in the bunk house.

I dug around until I found a can of food for Puck. I placed a small bowl on the ground and sat beside him, petting him while he ate, looking at the view. My spot by the creek wasn't bad. I could hear the sound of the rushing water. Besides, the parking lot was dead. There wouldn't be any noise.

After Puck had gobbled down his meal, he jumped in the cab, and we snuggled together on the small cot behind the seat. I pulled the curtain closed, and we called it a night.

CHAPTER TWO

I THOUGHT Red was going to wake me the next morning so I was surprised to see the sun was up when I pulled back the curtain. Puck whimpered to get out. I opened the door, and he bolted to the nearest tree. Mist was rising from the creek. It covered the parking lot and fairgrounds with thick fog. I pulled myself together, grabbed my tools, and Puck and I headed over to the Big Eli. Sometimes the boys tried to pamper me a bit, acting like substitute fathers. They probably decided to let me sleep and do the teardown alone. I wasn't having that.

Still sleepy, I wandered back down the midway toward the rides. The fog was so thick you could barely see your hand in front of your face. It helped a little that the lights were still on, though that was really weird. Maybe the electrician had gotten sick too. God knows Marx would never let the electricity run like that. Maybe he'd already headed out. The colorful lights cast a strange glow in the fog. It felt spooky.

As I turned down one of the aisles toward the rides, I thought I saw Beau's hulking figure standing in the row facing the other direction. He was just standing there between the lemonade stand and the sugar shack. I couldn't see him clearly in the fog. It looked like he had his back toward me; I only saw his outline. I was about to call out to him when Puck let out a very low and very serious growl. It was a sound I'd never heard him make before. I looked down to see Puck's ears were flat and his hackles up.

Beau turned and walked off in the other direction.

I firmed up my grip on my pipe wrench, and we headed toward the rides. When I got to the Big Eli, I was surprised to see no one was around. The ride was untouched. I stood there trying to decide what to do when I heard someone walking toward me. I could tell by the jingling sound that it was Vella; she always wore anklets with small bells.

"Hey Cricket," she called lightly. I could tell she was trying to sound cheerful, but I could hear the worry in her voice. She looked ready to go. While she still had her long, curly black hair covered in a scarf, she'd given up her colorful skirt for a pair of jeans and a red embroidered blouse. Kathy at the incense joint had started selling all kinds of embroidered shirts and dresses. Vella must have gotten the top there. Any time you saw Vella in jeans and out of "reader" gear, it was time to go.

"Guess no one else is up yet," I said, looking around. "Well, maybe Beau, but I'm not sure."

"I'm all packed. When are you heading out?"

"I was gonna go hook the truck up now since Red is still

snoozin'. He'll probably be up by the time I'm done. I need to help with the teardown, then we'll head out."

Vella's forehead crinkled with worry.

"What's wrong?"

"I think we better go. This flu . . ." she trailed off.

She was right. If everyone at the bunk was sick, no doubt we'd catch it too if we stayed around much longer. Puck trotted over to her and licked her hand.

"You agree, huh?" I asked the dog who wagged his tail at me.

"All right then. Let's go check on Mama Rosie, and then we can head out."

Vella nodded, and we walked back up the aisle to the snake show. Mama was outside. She had just rolled up the awning on the truck which was already running. Her forehead was dripping; she was soaked in sweat.

"You okay, Mama?" I asked.

She jumped. "Good lord, Cricket. You scared me. This mist is thick as pea soup. It's something, ain't it?"

"It sure is."

"We are walking in the shadow land," Vella said in a hollow voice.

I frowned; Vella's words spooked me. "Mama Rosie, you don't look like you're feelin' good."

"Ahh, Crick, that shrimp I ate yesterday had a wang to it. I knew I was gonna be in for a long ride, but I'll be fine. You two headed out?"

I nodded.

"I'll meet you at the exit," Mama said as she grabbed the van door handle.

"I already moved my Bronco to the west parking lot by your truck. I'll walk with you," Vella told me.

With a wave, Mama Rosie pulled the traveling snake show onto the aisle. Driving slowly, she headed toward the gate.

Vella and I traveled back to the parking lot. I noticed that Mr. Iago had already left. I was glad. The further away he was from me the better.

"I don't like him either," Vella said then stopped and grabbed my arm.

Coming out of the fog, there were about four people moving slowly down the aisle toward us. Just by the way they were walking, you could tell they were up to no good. Again, Puck growled that low, dangerous growl.

I felt like my skin was about to crawl off me. "Thieves?" I whispered to Vella.

"I don't know, but let's go," she whispered and pulled me between the duck pond and the t-shirt joint. We were headed down an aisle away from the figures when I turned and looked behind us. The figures were moving faster and coming in our direction.

"Stop a sec," I whispered to Vella.

"What? No way! Come on," she replied.

"Vella, your bells," I whispered to her, pointing to her ankles. The tinkling sound of her anklets had echoed through the fog as we fled.

Vella swore a slew in Romanian as she quickly kicked the anklets off.

We could see the figures coming closer toward us. For a

minute, I thought I saw someone wearing a hat just like Red's.

Vella pulled me by the arm.

"Wait, is that Red?" I whispered, looking back.

"Wouldn't Red call out?" Vella replied. "Come on," she said, pulling me again.

We ran between the booths and made our way to the gate. As we snuck through the fairground, we saw lots of people standing around in the fog. That was the odd thing. They were just standing there: not moving, not talking, just standing there. Every muscle in my body was pulled tight. They weren't thieves. They were something else.

Just as we turned the corner near the high striker, we ran into Beau.

"Beau? You all right? There are people all over the grounds. Something weird is goin' on!"

Vella took two steps back. Puck uttered a growl, showing his teeth.

Beau, who had been standing with his back to me, turned. His face had gone pale white. Strange frothy saliva leaked from his mouth. His chin was covered in blood, and his white t-shirt was also stained red. His eyes were a terrible milk-white color and red shot all through them like you see sometimes in an over-developed egg yolk. I gasped. Beau hissed, and then lunged toward me.

"Cricket, look out," Vella screamed.

I moved just in time. Beau stumbled over the machine and fell. He got up, slowly, and came at me again. I swiped him across the chin with the pipe wrench. His chin broke and hung slack. He looked at me and lunged again.

Puck jumped between us and growled, momentarily confusing Beau. I lifted the wrench again just in time to see Vella lift the high striker mallet and lower it onto Beau's head. There was a terrible cracking noise, and then Beau went down, blood pouring from his ears.

"Oh my God," I whispered, my hands shaking. "Oh my God, you killed Beau!"

"That. . .that wasn't Beau! Let's go!"

We bolted out of the gate and into the parking lot. I was headed toward my truck when Vella called to me. "No, Cricket! Look! There's no time." She was pointing back at the fairground. Ambling down the aisle toward the gate were at least a dozen people, all carnie folks we knew, who looked to be in the same condition as Beau. Red was at the front. Blood was smeared across his face. Every one of them looked like they were aiming to kill us. From somewhere in the park, I heard a woman scream. It sounded like Mrs. Chapman.

"But the tilt," I called to Vella.

"No, you'll never make it," Vella yelled. "Come on!"

"I can't leave it here!"

"Cricket, we've got to run or we're going to die!"

We both rushed toward her old Ford Bronco sitting just near the gate. Vella slid into the driver's seat and turned the ignition. Puck and I jumped in. Vella hit the gas, heading toward the fairground exit.

Mama Rosie was parked just near the exit when we came down to the road. Vella pulled up beside her.

"We've gotta get out of here, Mama. The flu got everyone, and they are all wild, trying to bite, and I don't know what. Christ, Beau tried to kill me. Look in your mirror. We've got to haul it," I told her.

I saw Mama Rosie look back to see the deranged-looking crew rushing after us. "Oh, my lord, let's go," she called.

We sped off. I turned on the radio. There was only one station broadcasting, and it was playing a recording of cities under quarantine.

"What the hell is goin' on?" I said, my eyes tearing up. Had Beau really tried to kill me? Had Vella just smashed his head in? What the hell!

"The Tower," Vella replied. She reached across the truck and opened the glove box, pulling out a map. "We need to get to the interstate," she said, handing the map to me.

I opened the map and quickly took a look. As we drove, I noticed a couple of cars had pulled over on the side of the road. It looked like people were sleeping inside. I scanned the map and found our location. "Left at the next turn," I told her. "It'll take us up to the ramp."

I set the map down and looked out. There was a car on fire on the road ahead of us. Vella slowed to pass it. In the cow pasture nearby were two figures, a woman and a child, both walking slowly.

"You think they're all right? You think they need help?" I asked Vella.

Vella just stared at them.

I rolled down my window. "Hey, y'all okay?" I called.

They turned and looked at us. They had that strange, sick look too. Their mouths were foaming. They ran toward us.

"Mother Mary," I whispered.

Vella took off.

I looked back to see that they had run up to the side of Mama Rose's van, but she was able to pull safely by.

When we got to the interstate on-ramp, we found it was completely jammed.

"What do we do now?" Vella asked.

I could see people sitting in their cars: men, women, children. Some men were standing outside their vehicles talking. Many of them were armed. Inside the large SUVS, small TV screens played cartoon movies, keeping kids otherwise frightened out of their wits calm. In the distance, I heard gun shots. "We gotta take to the back roads," I told Vella.

"But to where?"

"I don't know, but the more backwoods the road is, the better. Go that way," I said, pointing ahead. "Looks like there is an old country route ahead a ways."

I stuck out my arm and waved at Mama to follow us.

We drove down the road. It was fall, and the trees overhead made a canopy of red, yellow, and gold. The road before us was spotted with sunlight. We passed more cars pulled to the side. After we had gone a ways, we turned onto the old country route. Half dirt and full of potholes, no one had bothered to repave it in years. The road was rough but deserted. Vella's Bronco easily took on the rugged terrain, but I worried about Mama Rosie.

We had been driving for a few hours, trying the radio with no luck, when we finally came to a fork in the road. We had a choice between two dirt roads. We pulled over and examined the map. The Bronco was low on gas, and the small town that was supposed to be there wasn't. Vella's map was as old as her Bronco. There was no sign of a town or anything else anywhere. I had wanted to get away from people, but I didn't want to be in the middle of nowhere. Both roads looked equally country. We knew Mama Rosie's truck wouldn't be able to make the haul. She'd have to ride with us.

"Let me go talk her into coming with us," I said to Vella, opening the door.

"I can move some stuff and fit her in the back."

"It ain't her fittin' I'm worried about. What if she won't leave her snakes?"

"Convince her."

I nodded, and Puck and I hopped out and headed toward Mama's van.

When I came to the side of the van, Mama wasn't in the driver's seat. She must have gone back to check her snakes. I opened the door and called to her. "Mama Rosie?"

She didn't answer.

I looked down at Puck. He seemed nervous. He never liked Mama's snakes, and I didn't blame him. I stepped up into her truck. The door to the back of the van was open. I walked in to see Mama Rosie sitting at the ticket seat at the other end. I also noticed a couple of the pens had been opened.

"Mama, you all right? You got snakes out?" I called.

Mama Rosie didn't move. Only a little light showed in from the skylight overhead. Mama's head hung low.

I took two steps into the van. One of the snakes hissed at me, lunging at its glass cage wall.

"Mama?"

Puck was standing on the driver's seat dancing around nervously.

When I came up to Mama Rosie, she was still not moving. Her arms and legs hung limply. Her head hung low.

"Mama?" I said, and gently putting my hand on her forehead, I tilted her head back.

Her eyes rolled forward with a flutter. They were milk white. She opened her mouth, and a gurgling sound erupted. Two black snakes came slithering from her open mouth. She rose and lunged at me.

Puck started barking loudly.

I ran toward the front of the van, knocking several of the cages down behind me, blocking Mama's path. As I turned to leave, a snake darted out of in front of me. I jumped sideways and fell into the driver's seat. Mama Rosie was grunting and pushing through the cages. Puck barked at the snake and chased it out of the van.

I found myself staring down at the driver's side floor, face to face with one of Mama's tarantulas. It wandered away. Just then I remembered something. I jabbed my hand under the seat, praying to God no snakes were hidden there, and found Mama Rosie's handgun.

I pulled it out in time to see Mama Rosie come crashing toward me. I aimed as best I could, closed my eyes, and fired.

I heard Mama Rosie hit the ground with a thud.

A moment later, Vella came running up.

"Oh my God! Are you okay?"

I sat up to see I had shot Mama Rosie between the eyes. Snakes were crawling everywhere.

"Get out of there," Vella called, lending me a hand.

We closed the door to the van and stood at the side of the road breathing hard.

"You shot her in the head," Vella said.

I nodded, but I also started crying. My stomach flopped, and I turned to the weeds at the side of the road and threw up. I had shot Mama Rosie. My whole body shuddered as I thought about those snakes bursting out of her mouth. I threw up again. What the hell was happening?

"No, I mean, she went down when you shot her in the head. Beau, he didn't feel a thing when you hit him across the chin, but he went down when I bashed him on the head. There is something going on with the head, the brain. There's something about this flu and the brain."

I nodded, understanding. I wiped my nose on my shoulder, took a deep break, and stood up. "Where the hell are we?" I asked.

"Falling from the Tower," Vella replied.

I frowned. "Now, none of that. Come on. We need to get somewhere safe."

Vella frowned, making her dark eyes crinkle at the corners. "Where is safe now?"

She was right. Where could you hide?

CHAPTER THREE

VELLA and I hopped back into the vehicle. I backed the Bronco down the road and siphoned the gas from Mama's van. I hated to leave her there like that, but I wasn't going back in there with those snakes. We then turned down a dirt road, Forest Road 17, and headed into the woods. We drove for hours before we saw anything. Eventually, however, we came across *The Hickory Nut Camp Store*. We pulled the Bronco in beside the old gas pumps. They looked like antiques more than anything else. I lifted the rusted handle: I was right, no gas. The lights were on inside so we headed in—carefully.

"Hello?" I called, pushing the door open very slowly. I had Mama's gun, and my pipe wrench, and Vella was still carrying the mallet.

Static buzzed from the TV mounted on the wall behind the counter.

The store was full of all kinds of camping gear: tents,

lanterns, sleeping bags, and other odds and ends. I spotted a machete in a belt holder hung on a peg nearby. I pulled it from the rack and strapped it around my back.

"Anyone here?" Vella called.

Puck was braver than the two of us. He trotted into the store and started poking his nose into the shelves. It wasn't long before he'd torn into a bag of beef jerky. He sat down on the floor beside the soda cooler and chewed his lunch.

"Let me check the back. Grab some supplies?" I said to Vella who nodded.

I went around the counter toward the store room. "Hello? Anybody home?" I called.

A single light bulb lit the back room. It flickered off and on. The setting sun shone in through two very dusty old windows. I decided the place was clear and turned to head back to the front when I spotted the toe of a shoe sticking out into the aisle. Someone was sitting on the floor at the end of the row.

"Hello?" I called. My skin turned to goosebumps. When I didn't get an answer, I feared the worst. I whistled. A moment later, Puck appeared. With my Puck at my side, I carefully crossed the storeroom. Whoever was sitting there didn't move. When we got close, Puck stopped and sniffed the ground. He barked at the figure.

I raised the gun and stepped sideways to stand in front of whoever was sitting on the floor.

A man, maybe around fifty years old, was slumped sideways on the floor. A handgun lay beside him. I could see he had shot himself in the head. His brains, pieces of skull and hair, were splattered all over the boxes. Blood pooled on the floor and spread toward the wall.

"Sorry, friend," I said, lowering my gun. I picked up the dead man's handgun, wiping off the blood on my jeans, and then headed back to the front.

Vella was just returning from the Bronco when I came back.

"I was loading supplies. Everything okay?" she asked.

"Depends on who you ask. Store owner shot himself. He's dead in the back."

"That seems rash."

"Can't say I blame him. Better than gettin' eaten by a person or turnin' cannibal." I handed the store owner's gun to Vella. "It's empty. He musta only had one bullet. Hang on to it. Maybe we'll stumble across some ammo."

Vella nodded, stuck the gun into her bag, then she and I loaded up the Bronco with the rest of the supplies. We headed out. We tried to follow the map but we were so backwoods that it wasn't much help. By nightfall, we were completely lost. It didn't help much that Vella had only one headlight and no high beams. We drove through the woods and sometime around midnight, we emerged at a clearing that overlooked a valley. Something about the place, maybe the glow of the moon on the grass bending in the wind or the moon's silver light reflected on the small field pond, made it look almost magical. It seemed as good a place as any to stop. I slowed the Bronco and put it into park.

I looked across the horizon. Suddenly, I saw a very strange blue-green light in the field. At first I thought it was a firefly, but the light never went off. The orb of light bounced across the grass. I watched it for a moment. Puck barked.

"You see that?" Vella whispered.

"Yeah, I see it," I replied.

"What is it?" Vella asked.

"Swamp gas?"

"A wisp?"

I frowned at Vella.

The light bounced playfully in the field.

"I think we should follow it," Vella said. Her voice was thin and mystical. I didn't like it a bit.

"I don't know about that," I replied.

"Just follow it," Vella answered.

I sighed. I didn't really want to follow the light, but I was curious. I turned the Bronco onto the grassy field and followed the glowing orb. It bounced over the grass and down a hill. The light went into the thick woods where the Bronco couldn't follow.

"We should go after it," Vella said.

"Walk after it? Like hell," I replied. "You do know it's night? And you do know we are in the middle of nowhere? And you do remember there are zombie-lookin' things creapin' around everywhere, right?"

Vella watched the light. "We should follow it," she said again.

I clicked off the Bronco and turned to have a very serious discussion with Vella when Puck, who had been sitting quietly between Vella and me, suddenly crawled across Vella's lap and jumped out the window.

I saw his tail wagging as he bounded across the grass toward the glowing light.

"Dammit," I swore and jumped out of the Bronco. I grabbed the pipe wrench and Mama's pistol and went after the dog. "Puck!" I called, but he ignored me. He bolted across the grass following the blue light.

Vella was hot on my heels.

"Soon as I get him back we're goin' back to the Bronco," I told her.

Vella said nothing but kept pace with me. The dog and the light disappeared into the dark woods. When I reached the border between the field and the forest, I hesitated.

"Puck!" I called into the woods with scolding authority. "Puck!" I realized then that if I went around screaming, I was inviting trouble. "Damned dog," I grumbled, and stepping into the forest, I went after him. Vella followed.

We wove through the woods. I could see the blue light and the shadow of Puck following behind it. Suddenly, however, the light bounced up then dropped out of view. I spotted Puck sitting on a rise. The moonlight was shining down on him. "There he is," I pointed. Vella and I ran toward him. When we got close, I called him again: "Puck, come here, you bad dog."

Puck rose, wagging his tail, and jogged toward me.

Vella walked toward the rise where Puck had been sitting. No matter what, I was done following weird lights. "Let's head back." I turned to go, grabbing Puck by the collar.

"Cricket?" Vella called.

"Oh, no. I'm not chasing any more lights in the woods. Come on."

"No, wait. Look!"

With a sigh, I walked back toward the rise where Puck had been sitting. Down across the valley below us we saw the twinkle of light. "What is it?"

Vella shook her head. "I don't know. Looks like some kind of building."

We both stood there considering.

I looked down at Puck. He whimpered excitedly, his tail wagging. "No way," I told him. He whimpered.

"We should go. Maybe we'll find some help," Vella suggested.

"Or maybe we'll get eaten alive. Or worse."

"Worse than eaten alive?"

"You know what I mean."

"There is no way to know for sure unless we look. After all, the wisp brought us here. Don't you agree, Puck?" Vella ask the dog who tipped his head and wagged his tail at her in agreement.

"I don't know . . ." My stomach knotted into a fist. My gut was telling me to stay put.

"Look at the top of the building," Vella said then.

I sighed then looked, squinting to see. "A star?" It looked like there was a shining silver star on top of the building. "Maybe it's a Holiday Inn."

She shook her head. "No. It's *the* Star," she replied.

"What do you mean, *the* Star?"

"In the tarot deck. The Star always follows the Tower."

"And what does that mean?"

"Hope."

"If you say so," I said then sighed. "Lights can also mean a soft bed and a hot meal," I added, defeated. I stuck the pistol in the back of my jeans, and keeping a tight grip on my pipe wrench, gazed across the vista at *the* Star.

CHAPTER FOUR

VELLA and I crouched low in the underbrush at the side of the road. "I can't see anything," I complained in a whisper. All the street lamps were out. Only the stars and a bit of moonlight lit up the night. *Darker than a grave,* my daddy would have said, or *darker than the inside of a cow,* or *darker than a stack of black cats.* Daddy always had a way of saying things that made me laugh.

We were on the far side of an abandoned four-lane highway. There were no cars in sight. It was dead quiet. Across the street sitting on a hillside was a boarded up shopping center. Thin slants of light shone out from between the boards covering the windows of *Fisher's Big Wheel,* an abandoned big box store at the plaza's center. On the roof of the plaza was a radio tower. And on the top of that tower was a glowing star: blue-colored solar lights reflected off faded Christmas tinsel wrapped around a wire star.

"So much for your star," I told Vella.

"A star is a star. It's still a symbol."

I sighed. Vella and I had left the Bronco hidden in the forest. We'd headed out to follow Vella's hunch—mostly against my better judgment—on foot.

Vella started digging through her pack. "I found some binoculars at the camping store," she said, lifting the heavy black binoculars. She peered at the building. "I don't see anyone or anything outside, but something is moving inside. Now what?"

Just what I needed, to be led around a dying world by an uncertain fortune teller. "You're askin' me? If you've got cold feet, I say we head back to the Bronco. It was your—and Puck's—idea to come here. You tell me *now what*."

"Then we follow the Star. Let's go," she said then stood.

"And what if they aren't friendly?" I asked with a harsh whisper.

"But what if they are?"

"We shouldn't go around just trustin' anyone. They could be murderers, rapists, God-knows-what. And maybe they won't trust us either, and then where will we be?"

"We are two women and a dog. Besides. . .the Star."

"Yeah, yeah," I said with a frown. I checked Mama Rosie's pistol again. I only had five shots left. Finding some ammo was becoming a priority. I adjusted the hunting knife strapped around my chest. "Dammit!" One of the pink rhinestone bedazzles spelling the word *cute* on my tanktop fell off.

Moving quickly and carefully, we scooted across the highway. Puck dashed alongside us, his ears tilting back and forth; he was on full alert. From the way he was acting, I knew there was something nearby. I just wasn't sure if it was a living person, a raving cannibal, or a squirrel.

We ducked low when we reached the median. Since it looked clear, we headed across the grass and up the hill to the shopping plaza. There were six cars and a church van parked very close to the front door. Vella and I ran to the first car and dropped low. My heart was thudding in my chest. I didn't want it to show, but I was scared out of my wits. Not only might the people inside shoot us on sight, but what if one of those deranged-looking people came bursting out?

Vella, however, looked confident. Her dark eyes took in everything. I always thought that she looked at the world differently than the rest of us, like she saw more than the rest of us did. I sure hoped so.

"How do we get in?" I whispered. Up close, we were able to see that the front of the store was boarded up and covered with chicken wire. The doors were chained shut.

"Around back?"

"You sure about that?" The building was backed up against the side of the mountain. Surely there wouldn't be more than a single car's worth of width in the alley. Such a dark and narrow space sounded iffy on a normal day.

"Come on," she said confidently. Not waiting for my answer, she bent low and headed off toward the back of the building, Puck trotting quickly behind her. Neither of them looked back.

"Dammit," I whispered and took off after them. *Fool's errand*, my daddy would have said, *fool's errand*.

The long alley was shadowed by thick trees leaning over the roof. You couldn't see the other end. Not even a speck of moonlight shone there.

"I'm *not* goin' down there," I whispered harshly.

"There has to be a door. I have a flashlight."

"No way. I mean it. No way."

"We'll just use the flashlight."

"There is no way I'm goin' down there. Let's head back and scope it out again in the morning."

Before Vella could argue, we heard a grunt and the sound of footsteps coming from the alley. Someone or something groaned with a low gurgling sound that echoed off the plaza walls.

"Vella, go back," I whispered as I started to back toward the parking lot.

Vella paused to dig in her multicolored patched and embroidered satchel.

"Vella," I whispered, grabbing her arm, "let's go!"

Puck growled low and mean.

There was a dragging sound followed by a low groan. I tightened my grip on my pipe wrench and strained to look. Something was moving toward us. A soft wind blew down the alley. A horrid smell burned my nose: it stunk like a dead animal.

"There," Vella said, finally pulling her flashlight from her bag. She snapped it on just in time to shine it on one of the deranged-looking people lumbering toward us. He dragged his leg behind him.

Startled, Vella yelped, dropped the flashlight, and stumbled backward.

"Oh my God," I whispered. I pulled out Mama Rosie's gun and took aim as a man dressed in a bloody mechanics' jumper neared us. Blood dripped from his chin, staining his white undershirt. His eyes looked moon-white in the glow of the flashlight that had gone rolling toward the alley. The flashlight's beam cast spiraling light down the alleyway.

"Stay back!" I yelled. My hands were shaking.

"Shoot him!" Vella yelled.

I shook my head. I was no killer. Mama Rosie. . .I was scared. It was an accident. This wasn't the same thing. "Stay back, man. I don't wanna shoot you," I told him again. But still he came toward me. White frothy saliva tinged with blood poured like a fountain out of his mouth, and he moved quickly toward me. He bit and snapped. As he got closer, I smelled that terrible stench again. It was coming off him. He smelled like rotted meat and shit. I gagged.

"Shoot, Cricket!"

Puck growled; his teeth were bared.

I raised the gun, closed one eye to squint, just like I did every time I played *Water Gun Fun* at Freckles' game booth, and pulled the trigger.

The gun blasted causing an echoing ring down the alley. With a gurgling grunt, the man dropped. The gunshot had startled a flock of crows that had roosted in the tree overhead. They cawed in protest and flew away. I watched them swirl up into the night's sky.

I lowered the gun. For a split second, I felt relieved, but the moment passed because a second later, the alley erupted in sound. First we heard moaning. As if in slow motion, the flashlight on the ground rolled to a stop, the beam of light pointing down the alleyway. A horde of deranged-looking people lumbered toward the sound of the gunshot, toward us. The flashlight shined in their eyes, causing a mirror-like reflection. They began moving quickly toward us.

"Sweet baby Jesus," I whispered.

"Run!" Vella yelled.

Vella, Puck, and I turned from the alley to run back into the parking lot when another small group of six or so appeared behind us, blocking our path. They had snuck up on us from behind. Were they capable of sneaking? Where had they come from?

I turned and shot at a large man lumbering toward us. His intestines, dripping with brown ooze, slid out of a gash in the side of his stomach. A sharp smell like the stink of slime at the bottom of a trash bin wafted off him. The shot hit his shoulder but didn't slow him down.

"The head!" Vella shrieked. "Shoot him in the head!" A young woman lunged at Vella. Vella lifted the high-striker mallet and swung hard, smashing the girl on the side of the head. Blood splattered across Vella's shirt and jeans. The woman slumped to the ground. I lifted the gun again and shot once more as I tried to fall back, away from the horde of at least thirty creatures rambling out of the alleyway toward us. This time my shot hit home, clipping the large man across one side of his head. He fell to the ground, jerking wildly, like his body was hit with electric shock. Finally, he went still.

"Here! Up here!" I heard someone yell.

Vella and I looked around wildly.

"There!" Vella said, pointing.

On the roof of the plaza, I saw a man waving at us. He held flashlights in both of his hands.

"Try to get up here!" he yelled.

I scanned the side of the building. Halfway down the alley, between us and the horde lumbering toward us, the light from the flashlight showed the dim shadow of a fire escape.

Vella saw it at the same time. She pointed. "There, Crick!"

"We'll never make it!" I cast an eye all around. The limbs of a large oak tree on the hill behind the building extended over the roof. If we could get up the tree, we could drop down onto the roof. "There! There! Up the tree and over. Let's go," I said, pointing. I turned and started clambering up the grassy slope to the wood line.

Grunting and snapping, the deranged people advanced on us.

"Come on, Vella!" I called to her.

Vella turned and ran up the side of the hill, grabbing hand-holds of weeds to pull her up the steep bankside. A few minutes later, she was standing at the tree line. She jumped up, grabbed a tree branch, and pulled herself into the tree.

Puck had already climbed to the top of the hill and was standing under the tree, dancing nervously as he barked at the approaching horde.

I clambered up the hill behind them. By the time I got to the top, Vella was already working her way across the branches to the roof. From the looks of it, I started to suspect Vella had spent some time in the big top. Two of the sick looking people tried to climb up the hill after us. Their movements were slow and clumsy. I aimed at the woman closest to us. My shot hit its mark. She fell to the ground, knocking down two others.

I bent down and took Puck by the collar. "Baby, run. You understand me? I can't lift you, and you can't come after me. You gotta run. I'll find a way to get you in but run! Go, Puck! Run," I yelled at him, pointing into the woods behind us, away from the. . .zombies. That's what they were, weren't they? Zombies? I could barely believe it. The dog cocked his head to the side and looked at me.

"Run! Go," I yelled at him again. A moment later, Puck turned and ran into the woods. He disappeared out of sight. I grabbed the limb nearest me just as one of the zombies reached me. I heaved myself up, pulling with all my strength. The zombie grabbed my boot and pulled hard. I gasped as I felt him drag me down. I wrapped my arm around the branch, the bark biting my skin, and yanked my leg up as I wiggled my foot. With a tug, I pulled my foot out of my cowboy boot. It unbalanced him; he fell to the ground, knocking down several others coming up behind him. I climbed into the tree, grabbing limbs overhead to pull myself up and out of reach.

Moving carefully, Vella and I shimmied across the limbs of the tall oak tree toward the building. Vella balanced carefully, swinging one foot in front of the other as she made her way across. The man on the roof was waving us in, shinning his flashlight on the tree branches.

"Careful," he yelled. "Careful!"

"Vella, you okay?" I called to her.

She was stone silent as she moved her way across the branches.

We were nearly twenty feet above the alleyway, and the branches were thinning as they bent toward the roof of the building.

"Easy does it," I called to Vella again, who did not answer me.

I listened for Puck. No barks. No whimpers. He had just disappeared into the night.

My fingers gripped the gritty bark. Fear made my hands prickle. Below, the zombies reached toward us, their bloody mouths snapping. If we fell, we were done. My heart pounded in my throat. Though it was cool, sweat trickled from my brow. And to think, I could have spent the night sleeping cozied up to Puck in a nice thermal sleeping bag in the back of the Bronco. Instead, I was dangling from a tree like bait. My hands tingled, the feeling of pins and needles setting them on fire, as I crossed the branches. I was doing okay until my boot heel slipped. I hooked my arm around the tree limb to balance myself.

"Careful, Miss," the man yelled to me.

Vella had reached the thin branches above the building. She crouched down on the branch, grabbed the limb between her feet, then as slow as she could, she lowered herself. She was dangling maybe six feet above the roof. A moment later, she dropped safely onto the roof.

"Watch over me, Daddy," I whispered as I shimmied through the tree, trying to ignore the open mouths below me, waiting to gobble me whole. I moved across the branches until I reached the limb where Vella had dropped down. I bent and moved just like she did, dropping onto the roof.

I hit the roof with a thud, my foot still wearing the cowboy boot twisting when I landed. Sharp pain shot through my ankle. I yelped.

"Cricket!" Vella reached out for me.

"My ankle," I whispered.

"You're okay now, young lady," the man said, helping me up. I realized then that he was just a slip of a thing with thin white hair. His kind face was lined deeply, and he wore a pair of small glasses.

"Thank you," I told him as Vella pulled my arm across her shoulder and grabbed my waist to steady me.

"Any more of them down the alley? Is it clear the rest of the way down?" I asked the old man, breathing hard from the climb. My heart was slamming in my chest.

"They've been stuck back there all day trying to break into the back door. We've got it barricaded with a dumpster. You two flushed them out. They're all up here now," he said, pointing over the side of the roof.

We couldn't see the horde that had come of out of the alley, but we could hear their groans.

"The door. . .I left my dog out there. Maybe we can open it just a crack to let him in?"

"It's all barred up right now. We'll wait until morning. If they've cleared out, we can try."

I stared into the woods. Where was Puck? "Until morning?"

"There are people inside. We have to keep them safe. We can't risk the people inside for a dog," the old man said.

"He'll be okay. I promise you. He'll be okay," Vella said reassuringly. Vella looked up at the star twinkling at the top. "It's okay, Cricket. We're going to be fine now."

I wished I felt as sure.

CHAPTER FIVE

"COME ON, let's go inside. Got some folks downstairs. My wife and granddaughter. Some girls from our church. Couple people from off the road. Nice folks. Come on. You're all right now. I'm Elias," the tiny old man said.

I stared into the dark forest. My hands were shaking. Puck.

"Can you walk?" Vella whispered.

I nodded, turned, and limped alongside her to a door that led to the stairs below.

"Thank you so much. She's Cricket. I'm Vella."

"You girls on foot?" Elias asked as he opened to door to the stairs.

"Our car broke down," I lied.

"You're lucky then. How'd you come by us?" Elias asked as we entered the stairwell. Vella went ahead of me. Of course I would lose my boot. And of course the sock I had on had a massive hole in the bottom. The metal grooves on the stairs jabbed my bare heel.

"We saw the Star," Vella said. Her voice echoed as we moved through the darkness down the stairs. There was a lantern waiting at the bottom of the steps. Elias picked it up.

"My wife's idea. She figured folks would know to follow a star, just like the wise men. We boarded the shop up twenty years ago. Never sold the building. I was hoping *Walmart* would come along and buy me out. No luck. Just a big space full of boxes of junk no one ever wanted. Now I'm sure as hell glad I have it. Got flushed out of our house," he explained, his voice faltering at the end. He coughed, clearing his throat, but I heard the sadness in his voice. "Lost my daughter and her husband, but we made it here."

"I'm sorry," Vella told the old man, setting her hand on his shoulder.

"Me too," I added.

"Whatever this thing is, it's killing people fast. The whole country is sick," Elias said. We emerged into the storage room. It was dark and cavernous. On the far end of the building, it looked like someone had made a fortress out of boxes. Thin light shone out.

"Honey, that you? You okay? I thought I heard gun shots," an old woman's voice called. I saw her silhouette in the dim light. She was a frail little thing, her hair tightly permed just like any other old lady.

"Got two girls here," Elias called back.

"How?" someone else asked. A man came out of the shadows and stood behind the old woman.

"Damnedest thing, climbed the trees and dropped onto

the roof!" Elias answered with a laugh as we crossed the cold cement floor toward them.

"Those bad people can't do that, can they grandma?" a little voice asked from the darkness.

"No, honey, I don't think so."

We rounded the corner to see that inside the little cardboard fort there were eight other people: Elias' wife, a little girl about five years old, the middle aged man who had spoken, two young men, and three teenage girls who were sitting on the floor. They had dragged a moth-eaten, pea-green couch into the small space.

"Come in, girls. I'm Gemma," Elias' wife introduced herself. "This is my granddaughter Katy."

"Hi!" Katy squeaked out.

"John," the big man said.

The two young men, both about my age, traded a glance then looked at us. "Chase," the one with the long dreadlocks said.

"Darius," his bald-headed friend added with a nod.

One girl with long, black hair who had been busy picking at the blue paint on her fingernails looked up at us. "Ariel," she said with a distracted smile.

A girl with red, puffy eyes smiled weakly at me. "I'm Jess. This is my sister Missy," she said, looking down at the girl who lay with her head in Jess' lap.

"Cricket. Vella," I introduced us.

"My mom and dad still out there?" Jess asked Elias as she stroked her sister's hair.

Elias shook his head and looked away. "It was real dark."

"I heard gun shots," Missy said, sitting up. "Did you. . .did you shoot any of them? The people outside?" Her voice was a jumble of sadness, fear, and angry accusation.

I looked at Vella. Good lord, had I shot their parents? I frowned. "I. . .only when they tried to grab me."

"What'd they look like?" Missy demanded.

"Missy, it's real dark out there," Elias cut in.

Jess was looking at Vella. "Is that blood on your clothes?"

"Girls, it was real dark outside, and these girls barely made it alive. You know your mom and dad aren't. . .well, they aren't right. It was dark. Besides, they may have wandered off by now."

Missy moaned terribly and collapsed back into her sister's lap again. Tears streamed down Jess' cheeks but she didn't ask any questions, and she didn't look at us again. She just sat stroking her sister's hair. Ariel gave us an understanding half-smile and went back to chipping the blue paint off her fingernails.

"You need to turn off that light," Chase said then. His voice was firm. I could tell it wasn't the first time he'd suggested it. "You're just waving in trouble."

"We're no trouble," I told him.

"Not you, Miss," Chase told me with soft smile. "But people are running scared and running red. We saw things," he said, glancing at Darius who nodded. "You need to turn off that light."

Gemma shook her head. "The Lord will lead the meek to the star. Now, enough of this," she said, ending the conversation. "Come in girls. Sit down."

Vella and I took a spot on the floor. John sat beside us. He picked up a radio sitting on the boxes then switched it on. He scanned through the stations. There was no live radio, just recordings of quarantine in what sounded like every city in the United States.

"The beginning of the end," Darius said then.

"Just doom and gloom," John agreed and switched the radio off. We all sat in silence. Outside, we could hear the faint moans of the deranged. . .zombies. . .trying to find a way inside.

"Like the plagues of Egypt," Gemma said. "Should we sing? 'Let there be Peace on Earth?' 'Onward Christian Soldiers?' What do you prefer?" Without waiting for an answer, she started singing: "Let there be peace on Earth, and let it begin with me . . ." Gemma began, but when no one joined her, not even her husband, she went silent. She sat down on the floor and picked up her granddaughter, cradling the small girl against her chest.

Silence filled the space again. No one spoke a word.

CHAPTER SIX

"ALL CLEAR," Elias said.

It was morning and Elias, Chase, Darius, Ariel, Vella, and I were standing at the front of the store looking through the wood slats barricading the windows. Dim sunlight shone in through the dusty glass. We scanned the parking lot. There were none of the zombie-looking people in the front. The parking lot and highway outside were silent.

It had been a strange night. Against my better judgment, I'd fallen asleep. I dreamt of Puck. In my dream, I was chasing him through the woods. Again, he was running after the blue light. This time, however, we came to the gates of a massive old castle with high walls. The gate was flanked with two huge stone dogs that looked just like Puck. Behind me, I heard a noise. I looked back to see a huge horde of zombies lumbering toward me. Red, Mama Rosie, and Mr. Iago, except Mr. Iago looked exactly the same, were at the front of the zombie horde. Turning, I grabbed the bars of the gate and started screaming for someone to let me in. I realized then, however, that Puck was already sitting on the other side. I was all alone, the zombies advancing on me. I'd woken with a jolt.

"Clear out there. Let's head up to the roof and have a look around," Elias said, jostling me from my thoughts.

We crossed the white tile floor of the department store. The place was almost completely empty except for yellowed white plastic hangers hanging off clothes racks, dusty mirrors, a broken sign pointing to the layaway area, and a row of rusty shopping carts. Dust was piled up in the corners. At one end of the store was a stack of boxes full of donations intended for Elias' and Gemma's church. That morning, Gemma found me a pair of old work boots from inside. They were men's boots, but they fit well. I was still hoping to find my other cowboy boot outside. I loved those boots.

"Where are you headed now, honey?" Gemma asked when we came back.

"Roof," Elias replied. "Need to see if they moved out."

"My dog is still outside somewhere," I blurted out, feeling stupid the moment I said it. Those poor girls' parents were out there, infected, and I was worrying about my dog. But I loved Puck. He was my best friend. I couldn't expect nice people like Elias and his wife, who were probably used to big Sunday night dinners and family picnics, to understand that. Now that my daddy was gone, all I had was Puck and the tilt. And now the tilt was gone. I couldn't lose Puck too.

Gemma smiled sympathetically at me, tilting her head to one side, but she didn't say anything.

"We'll find him," Vella whispered. "Don't worry."

"I want to come," Jess said then, standing up. Her sister was still asleep on the couch. She had cried herself to sleep. It was heart-breaking.

Elias shook his head. "Best we have a look first."

"But my Mom and Dad. . .I want to see . . ."

"Best let us have a look first," Elias said again, but this time with authority, motioning for his wife to come between us and the girl.

"But Ariel—"

"Ariel is four years older than you, Jess. We'll let you know what we see."

We headed back to the stairs leading to the roof.

"You took down her daddy last night," Elias told me when we were out of earshot. "Don't want the girls to see. It wasn't your fault. I saw what happened. We understand, but she won't. Don't say anything to her, Ariel."

"No, sir," the girl said.

I looked back at her. She was following Vella up the stairs. Her gaze met mine. She shrugged sympathetically.

I turned back. My stomach rolled. "I'm so sorry," I whispered.

"If you don't get them, they'll get you," Chase said from behind me.

"Poor girls," Elias said then. "Their mom went bad first. It was all we could do to get Margie thrust out the back door without those little girls following after her. Their dad wouldn't listen. He pushed us aside and followed his wife out. The second he reached her, she bit a chunk right out of his neck. Horrible. Girls didn't see. They don't know. Don't understand."

"Does anyone understand?" I asked.

"Not me," Elias replied.

"What about the government? Are there any shelters? We didn't hear anything on the radio. Is the National Guard or Army out?" I asked.

Chase laughed. "Army? Darius and me took up with the Army day before last. We got pinned down with four other guys in a soup kitchen. Things went south. The Army guys locked us in a room with the zombies. . .fed us to them. . .so they could escape. Me and Darius got out. We were lucky. You can't trust anyone, which is why you need to turn off that light."

Elias nodded. "I'll talk to Gemma again."

We exited out onto the rooftop. The bright daylight made my eyes squint. Outside, it was quiet except the whistle of a cardinal perched in the trees overhead. He ruffled his red feathers as he settled in on the branch, blending in with the leaves that were turning the same color red as him. Fall had come. Carnival season would be over soon, except down south, not that it mattered anymore. I'd been looking forward to the jump to Cocoa Beach this winter.

"Stay back a minute," Elias said then made his way to the edge of the roof. The old man moved quietly, peering over the side. "Just Margie down there," he said. "Girls' mom."

Why would the girls' mom be there but the rest wander off?

We joined Elias at the edge of the roof. The woman he'd called Margie was standing in the middle of the alley, not moving.

"We'll check around the corner," Chase said, and then he and Darius set off toward the end of the building. Chase's handgun stuck out of the back of his jeans. I smirked; it was a nice view. *Not now, Cricket*! I scolded myself. I took a deep breath, refocused, and then looked into the woods. There was no sign of Puck anywhere.

"I need to go look for my dog," I told Elias. "It's quiet. I can sneak out the back and into the woods."

"Those. . .things. . .might have gone into the woods," Ariel told me. "And there is a big apartment complex on the other side. If you go too far, you might run into more."

"He'll come back, Cricket. We can wait for him," Vella reassured me.

"I'll take you," Ariel said as Darius and Chase returned. "We can go fast, look around really quick. The two of us could go quiet."

"Go where?" Chase asked.

"Her dog. He ran off into the woods last night."

"Miss Ariel, I don't think your parents would want me to let you run off on a fool's errand," Elias said.

Fool's errand. My daddy's words again.

"My parents are dead. At least I can try to help her. I know the woods here. We used to play in there," Ariel replied. "Cricket and I can go and come back quickly."

"I'll go with them. We need a look around, see if we can find supplies," Chase said. "You got anymore bullets?" he asked me.

"One."

"One isn't enough. Though, with that big ass knife, I suppose you'll be all right," Chase said with a grin.

"You for real? You're going after a dog?" Darius asked Chase.

"Just giving the girls a hand," Chase replied with a sly smile.

Darius rolled his eyes.

"Well," Elias said, running his hand through his thinning white hair, "I suppose you could go quick and come back. Gemma isn't gonna like it, but if you come back in one piece she won't nag me too much," he said with a chuckle.

I smiled at him and set my hand on his shoulder. "We'll be back soon."

We did one more scan from the roof. Besides the girls' mother, who didn't even seem to notice we were there, the rest of the deranged people were gone. We headed back to the stairs.

"I'll wait on the roof," Darius said, "and keep an eye out for you."

"I'll wait with you," Vella told him then turned to me. "Be careful," she said. "In the deck, the fool always has his dog at his side, but he is never careful enough. You'll find him, but watch yourself."

"I'm more interested in watching Chase's butt."

Beside me, Ariel snickered.

"Cricket!" Vella whispered back harshly. She reached out to take me by the shoulder, but when she did, her bag slid down her arm, and one of her tarot cards slid out.

I bent and picked it up. "The Moon," I said, handing it back to her.

Vella took the card from me and looked at it. "The Moon," she whispered, like she was talking to herself out loud. Vella stared me straight in the eyes, her dark eyes peering into mine. "If anything happens, trust your instincts."

I nodded, but all the hair on the back of my neck stood up straight.

Elias, Chase, Ariel, and I headed back downstairs. I turned and looked one more time at Vella. She clutched the tarot card in her hand, pressing it against her chest. We entered the stairwell. Elias shut the door tightly behind us, cutting off my view.

"There is another door at the very end of the plaza," Elias told us when we reached the store room. Taking out a massive key ring, he led us to a door at the back. He unlocked an old metal door. It opened with a creak. There was a long, dark hallway that led the length of the shopping plaza. "This way," he said, leading us deeper into the alley. "There used to be a pizza joint at the end of this strip. They had a side door for their dumpster. It's closest to the woods. We'll go out there."

Elias pulled a flashlight off his belt and flashed it down the hallway. It was cold and dark inside. The tiles overhead had fallen making mountains of wet, asbestos dust on the floor. Water dripped slowly from the ceiling. The concrete floor was wet.

"Anything left in the restaurant?" Chase asked.

That morning we'd eaten animal crackers and drank

liquid diet shakes for breakfast. Damned things had been sitting around for years but were still good even though they tasted like chocolate and chalk dust mixed together. Elias and Gemma had fled in their church van which had been loaded with food intended for a homeless shelter. We had supplies, but they weren't going to last more than a week or two.

"Well, if you count plastic flowers and sugar packets, then yes."

We reached the door at the end of the building. It was chained up. Elias unlocked the padlock holding the door closed. He carefully unsnaked the chain from around the door. Elias and Chase pushed on the door. It was sticky, but after a moment, it popped open.

"Be careful," Elias whispered. "Don't take any chances. Just do a quick look around then come back. Cricket, Chase, we need your help here," he whispered looking behind him.

Understanding, I nodded. If Chase was right, it wasn't just the zombies we had to worry about. And a little old man wouldn't be much of a fight for man or zombie.

Quickly and quietly, the three of us headed outside and darted across the alley. Margie didn't stir. We followed Ariel into the woods. Ariel stopped, however, once we were deep among the trees.

"Okay," she said, "the apartment building is about half a mile that direction. Don't get too close to it. I'll meet you guys back at the *Big Wheel* in a bit. Good luck finding your dog," she said and turned and headed in the other direction.

"Wait, where in the hell are you going?" I called to her.

"My boyfriend lives about a mile away. I haven't heard from him since cell service went down."

"Hold up, shorty. Don't go running off alone. Those things will eat you alive," Chase said.

"I'm fast. I run track. I'll go and bring Brian back."

"And what if your man is sick?" Chase asked.

"Then I'll come back alone."

I frowned then turned to Chase. "What about you? You got an agenda too?"

"Naa," he said with a grin. "I just like how you look with that big ass knife strapped around you. Don't want to see nothing happen to you."

I grinned, my heartbeat quickening. For a split second, I imagined twirling my finger around one of his dreadlocks. *Not now!* "Wait, Ariel. We'll come too."

Fool's errand. Suddenly everything felt like a fool's errand.

CHAPTER SEVEN

"TEENAGE LOVE," Chase mumbled under his breath. "Nothing burns hotter than teenage love."

"Oh, there are a few things hotter," I replied with a wink.

Chase grinned. I noticed that his cheeks dimpled when he smiled. Adorable.

Chase and I hustled behind Ariel. The girl moved through the woods in a hurry. The forest was thick, and thankfully, we didn't see a soul. It was dead quiet. The cardinal had stopped singing, and there was a strange feeling in the air, like the feeling you get right after a big lightning storm. The air buzzed with electricity.

"Puck," I whispered harshly as we moved through the woods, keeping an eye out for him as we went. Bad dog, didn't he know the world was coming to an end? Where had he gone? No doubt he was curled up under a bush in the dry leaves somewhere, snoozing the morning away. I didn't want to think of a worse alternative. "Puck!"

We climbed over a rise to see a small blue house sitting at the edge of the woods. There was an above-ground pool in the back. The water inside was green and full of leaves. The two-story house had a big deck in the back with a grill and an umbrella table. It was a nice place, typical townie house. But it looked cozy, like the kind of place where you could hole up with a man, have a few babies, watch sitcoms every night while you munch on popcorn, and drink beer.

"Brian's parents have a storm cellar," Ariel said. "There," she added, pointing to wooden double doors at the side of the house. "If they are going to be anywhere, they are going to be down there."

"Let's go," Chase said, pulling out his gun.

I pulled mine as well, knowing all too well I only had one shot left.

We sprinted across the lawn. There was no one around.

Ariel went straight to the storm cellar doors. "Brian?" she called, knocking on the wooden door. "Brian! It's Ariel! Mr. and Mrs. Clark, you inside?"

There was no answer.

"Brian?" Ariel called again.

Chase and I looked around as Ariel called out. Suddenly, I got this funny tingly feeling. All the hairs on my arm and the back of my neck stood up.

"Chase," I whispered.

Chase scanned around, gun ready.

Sheets hanging on the nearby clothesline snapped in the wind. A moment later, I saw it, the shadow of a person standing on the other side of the clothes line.

"Ariel," I whispered harshly, signaling to both her and Chase.

Ariel turned toward us, catching sight of the person standing by the clothesline. "Mr. Clark?"

"Shh!" I hushed her.

The figure didn't move.

Ariel took a step forward.

"No. Don't," Chase told her.

"Mr. Clark?"

He burst through the sheets, lunging at Ariel.

"Mr. Clark! No! It's Ariel," she shrieked and jumped back toward us. Red blood smeared the pretty white and pink sheets as Mr. Clark, his face, chin, and shirt covered in blood, lunged toward Ariel, his mouth wide open, teeth snapping.

Chase fired. His shot echoed across the valley. It was too loud. Mr. Clark dropped to the ground. Chase had shot him in the head.

"Oh, no," Ariel screeched and ran toward the man.

"No! Don't touch it!" Chase grabbed her just before she dropped to her knees beside him. "On the radio it said not to touch them."

I heard a groan behind me.

I turned in time to see a middle-aged woman with short blonde hair advancing on me. She didn't even have a shirt on, just a bra. She had a very large gash in the side of her face.

"Joelle," Ariel called.

I unhooked my knife.

"Get back," I told the woman. Her moon-white eyes

held steady on me. Just like Mama Rosie, she looked dead. Her face was pale, almost bluish at the edges, and froth dripped from her mouth.

"Joelle! No!" Ariel yelled.

Joelle lunged toward me. I lifted the big knife and swinging as hard as I could, swiped it toward her head. My arms shook when they felt the blade strike bone. Blood splattered across my shirt. Dammit! Joelle grew still; the blade stuck in her head. I let go. She fell onto the ground. I leaned over and put my boot on her chest, suddenly feeling conscious and careful not to step on her breasts, as I pulled the blade out. Blood and bits spilled from her head. I nearly threw up.

"Why'd you let her get so close?" Chase asked, coming up behind me.

"The gun makes too much noise, and I've only got one bullet."

"We need to go inside! Maybe Brian is trapped," Ariel said anxiously. Tears were streaming down her face. Without waiting for us, she turned and ran for the porch. Chase and I dashed behind her.

"Ariel, wait!" I called.

The screen door banged shut behind her. "That boy is going eat her alive. She doesn't have a sense of things yet," Chase said.

"Does anyone?"

"Well, nobody's going to take a chunk out of me. I'm too mean to eat."

"I find that hard to believe," I replied, but then I forced myself to switch my attention. There were zombies around, and I was still cruising for fun. What the hell was wrong with me? "Ariel," I called as Chase and I headed to the porch.

Moments later, we heard a scream coming from inside.

"Ariel," Chase yelled.

We ran into the house and followed the sound of Ariel screaming. There, lying on the living room floor, was what was left of Brian: a mangled lump of meat, two converse sneakers, a torn blue t-shirt, and a jaw, the teeth glimmering in the sunlight. The flies had already started to work on what was left of the corpse.

Ariel turned and threw up animal crackers, chocolate drink, and stomach acid all over the beige leather couch. The puke hit the couch with a splash that sent drops of vomit spraying back all over the girl. The smell of everything turned my stomach. I went back into the kitchen to catch my breath. I heard Chase speaking in low tones to Ariel who moaned.

I grabbed a dish towel, opened one of the bottles of water sitting on the table, and wet the towel. When I turned, Chase was leading Ariel back into the kitchen. Wordlessly, I handed the girl the towel and the water.

She wiped off her face and tried to sip the water, but the second after she drank, her stomach revolted again. She leaned into sink and threw up again.

"Any more people in the family? There a chance we might find someone else?" Chase asked her nervously.

"No," she whispered between wretches.

The sharp scent of stomach acid burned my nose, but I gently patted Ariel's back and stayed beside her. How many times had Mama Rosie held my hair back for me while I puked my guts out the morning after a bender. I think I must have stayed drunk for a solid month after my daddy died.

"Ariel, do they have any guns here?" Chase asked. "Whatever happened to them happened fast. Maybe they still have some ammo."

She threw up again then took a deep breath, wiped her face off, and nodded. "Upstairs. Mr. Clark kept a gun in his nightstand."

Chase turned and went upstairs while I eyed the open cupboards. They were full of canned soup, tomato paste, ramen noodles, and other supplies. I scanned around to see a backpack lying by the door. I picked it up and emptied the contents on the table then started filling the bag with supplies. Ariel turned and looked at the table. She picked up a piece of paper that had been inside the backpack.

"Homecoming registration," she said, looking at the paper. "The homecoming dance is next week. We were going to go together. My mom bought me a teal-colored dress. We were supposed to be on homecoming court, me and Brian. Did you go to your homecoming?" she asked me.

I shook my head. I didn't want to tell her my daddy homeschooled me, if you would call teaching a girl how to repair motors homeschooling, until I got my GED. I always felt a little embarrassed about the fact that I didn't even have a high school diploma when I was around truly educated people.

"Yeah, I guess I won't be going either," she said, tossing

the paper back onto the table. She cast a glance toward the living room then started weeping softly, her shoulders shaking.

Chase came back downstairs. "Got it," he said, eyeing my pack. "Even some spare bullets. Mr. Clark's gun was the same as yours, Cricket," he said, handing the box of bullets to me. "Isn't that lucky?"

"There is no such thing as luck," Ariel said harshly, wiping her tears.

I set the box of bullets on the counter then reloaded Mama Rosie's gun. I stuffed a handful into my pocket then put what was left into the backpack.

"I'm real sorry, Ariel, but we better go now," I said, picking up the backpack.

Ariel cast one long glance back toward the living room. I pitied her. No one should ever see someone they loved die like that. Ever. I was glad I'd never loved anyone, at least romantically, the way she must have loved him. Never did. Never will. But once more, I heard my daddy in my head: *never say never.*

CHAPTER EIGHT

ARIEL WEPT QUIETLY to herself as we made our way through the forest. I could hear her sniffling, but she didn't complain.

"Puck?" I called when we got deeper into the woods. "Damned dog. Puck!"

I climbed a rise in the forest to get a better view. To the left, I saw a thicket. If I were Puck, that's where I would have spent the night.

"Puck!"

I saw movement in the thicket then heard a little bark.

Chase and Ariel stopped.

"You hear that?" I called to them.

Chase and Ariel climbed the rise to join me.

"Puck!" I called again.

Again, a little bark came from the thicket.

"He must be stuck on something, otherwise he'd come," I said then headed toward the thicket, Chase and Ariel following behind.

Foolish dog. In the middle of all this mess, I was chasing my dog through the woods. The thicket was a tangle of rhododendron bushes and blackberry briars. The blackberry bushes were thick with fruit.

"Puck?" I whispered harshly.

There was a soft yelp in reply. My stomach filled with butterflies. Was he hurt?

"I'll go in. Don't want him getting spooked."

"We'll grab some of these while we wait. Katy will like them." Ariel said. She pulled off the scarf she'd been using for a belt and started picking berries.

Chase looked at both of us like we were crazy then, with a sigh, started helping Ariel.

Cursing under my breath, I pushed into the thicket.

"Puck, it's me. I'm comin', buddy."

I heard a whimper.

I pressed through the bushes. The thorns scraped my skin, the branches pulling my hair. The scratches itched and burned then grew bloody. I finally struggled through the tangle to pop out in a small opening in the middle of the briars.

For a moment, for just a split second, I thought I saw. . .a man. He was sitting on the ground, his legs crossed. The sunlight shined down on his dark hair. He looked up at me from under heavy eyebrows, the sunlight shining on his golden eyes, making them sparkle. What the hell? Then the wind blew, shifting the canopy overhead. I looked up. A beam of sunlight blinded me, making me wince. When I opened my eyes again, Puck was sitting there. There was no man, only the dog. Maybe I was hungrier than I thought.

"You bad dog! Didn't you hear me calling you?"

Puck whimpered and rose to walk toward me. He was limping. I bent down and lifted the paw he was nursing. There was a big thorn stuck inside.

"You big baby," I told him as I gently pulled the thorn away. "People are gettin' eaten alive, and you are whinin' over a thorn in the paw." I had to admit, it was in pretty deep. When I pulled it out, he whimpered and a little blood came out.

"Come on, you. Let's get you back, and I'll wash it up," I said as I scratched him on the head. "The things I'll do for love."

Puck licked my face.

"Spoiled rotten. I've probably got a hundred more scratches than you just chasin' in here after you," I scolded him, but I was also filled with relief. Heaven forbid I'd found him in the same state as Brian. I don't know what I would have done!

"Got him," I said as I emerged through the brush, Puck coming out behind me, nursing his injured paw.

Ariel smiled. I noticed the dark rings under her eyes. She was feeling miserable, that was for sure, but she was trying to hold herself together.

Chase grinned, shaking his head. "Let's get the hell out of here."

We headed back to the plaza. The forest was eerily quiet. Something felt strange. Something was off. When we got back to the plaza, we discovered that neither Darius nor Vella were on the roof. The fire escape had been lowered. Margie, the girls' mom, was lying dead in the alley. The dumpster had been pushed from the back door. A truck was parked near the back. From inside the building, I heard shouting followed by a gunshot then another.

Chase and I dropped to the ground. Ariel rose to go forward, but Chase grabbed her, pulling her down. Slowly, we moved back into the cover of the trees.

Two more trucks came speeding into the back of the alley, running over the body of Margie without a second thought. Her head smashed open like a grape. In the back of each truck were several armed men who jumped out and headed inside. From inside, I heard more gunshots ring out.

I closed my eyes. Vella! All those little girls! My whole body felt like it went stiff with shock.

Chase took a deep breath and clenched his jaw.

"There are so many of them!" Ariel breathed in alarm. "What do we do?"

"Darius is in there," Chase whispered harshly.

"If Darius is in there, he's probably . . ." Ariel started but didn't have the heart to finish.

Vella.

Puck whimpered and moved further back into the woods.

"We. . .we can't help. They might kill us too. We need to get out of here," Ariel said.

"Darius. . .and your girl, Vella, she might be. . ." Chase began, but then we heard two more gunshots.

"What can we do? We're just three people. There must be a dozen of them. But those girls," I whispered. "Maybe we can—" I began, but then Puck growled low and dangerous.

Seconds later, we heard a scream. Gemma ran out into the alleyway. Her face was a bloody mess. A man appeared in the doorway behind her holding a rifle. With a laugh, he shot her in the back. When she fell, he shot her again in the head.

There was commotion from inside, and for a moment, we could hear Katy's cry on the wind.

"Shut that brat up!" the man yelled to someone inside.

A blast sounded from inside. We didn't hear Katy again.

"Oh my God," Ariel breathed. "Oh my God. We need to go. Those girls were my friends, but we need to go," Ariel said as she began tugging on my arm.

My gut kept nagging me. Suddenly, I knew Vella wasn't in there. She wasn't there, and neither was Darius. "The fire escape was down. Vella and Darius. . .they may have gotten away. The Bronco," I said then, gazing back at Puck. "Vella and I lied. We have an SUV, about three miles into the woods across the road from here. We came over to check this place out. We followed the star. Vella and Darius were not on the roof. If they got away, that's where she went."

"Let's go," Ariel said then led us back into the woods. "There is a culvert half a mile down the road at Moon Creek. A big pipe leads under the road to the other side. We can go through there. No one will see us. It pops out in the woods. Can you find your way back to the SUV?"

"Did you say Moon Creek?"

"Yeah. Can you find your way back?"

"I'll sure as hell try. Let's go."

CHAPTER NINE

ARIEL, Chase, and I headed through the woods to Moon Creek. We could still hear ruckus coming from the shopping center behind us, but my instincts were screaming at me to run.

"This way," Ariel said, leading us down a sloping hill. In the distance, I could hear a rushing stream. "Moon Creek is in the valley. Brian and I used to go fishing there."

My heart was racing as we made our way through the woods. Puck bounded off ahead of us to the stream, stopping to drink when he got to the water's edge. The hill was steep. Steadying myself, I made my way to the water. The fallen pink-colored pine needles made the ground slippery. More than once my boot slipped, but I grabbed a tree trunk in time to keep from falling. It was no wonder I couldn't keep my footing; my knees were shaking. What had I just seen? Elias! Those poor girls! I felt angry and powerless. All I could do was run and hide, but it felt wrong. I didn't want to abandon them. But. . .they were already dead. I fought back tears as I dragged along behind Chase and Ariel.

"Let's go," Ariel said, leading us upstream toward the highway. I could make out the overpass. There was a massive culvert under both lanes of highway. It was perfectly secluded, but we'd have to get wet to pass underneath. Moving quick, Ariel, followed by Puck, went to the culvert entrance.

"Is it deep?" Chase called. I saw a flicker of worry cross his face. I didn't blame him. I wasn't keen on getting wet either.

"No more than knee-high but probably cold," Ariel replied then stepped into the water. It swallowed her foot and half her leg, her sneakers disappearing under the waves.

Chase went in behind her. "Oh, hell no!"

Puck edged into the side of the culvert, prancing practically sideways as he tried to make his way through without swimming. His nimble feet carried him fast; he dashed ahead of us.

I slogged in behind them. The chill of the water hit me hard: it felt like ice shot up my spine. Water filled my boots. I shuddered. My heart was beating so loud I worried I'd have a heart attack. The culvert was a massive metal pipe maybe fifteen feet in diameter. Inside, it was dark, and the water was congested with a tangle of weeds, sticks, shopping bags, soda cans, and other garbage. The water snaked slowly through the clogs. The whole place smelled fishy.

"Gross," I whispered. Looking ahead, I saw that Puck had already maneuvered himself safely through the culvert.

He was standing on dry land on the other side, looking back at us like he was wondering why we were taking so long.

Ariel was moving around a pile of twigs and trash. I saw her step carefully among the branches when suddenly she seemed to have trouble pulling her leg free. She jerked her foot, but it was stuck. A second later, she shrieked. "Oh my God! Something is pulling on my leg!" She tugged, trying to pull herself free.

Chase and I ran to her. He bent down to help her. A hand, the skin faded to white and blue, reached out of the water and grabbed Chase by the shirt sleeve. Just under the water, covered by the litter, I saw the flash of white eyes and teeth.

Chase yanked his arm back, ripping his shirt as he tore himself free.

"Help," Ariel screeched. The water cleared, and I saw a white hand wrapped around her ankle.

Chase pulled out his gun.

"No!" I said, pushing down the barrel. "You'll deafen us, and the bullet might bounce. . .not to mention, the people at the plaza could hear." Taking hold of Chase to steady myself, I stomped hard on the face submerged underwater. Again and again I stomped until I felt a weird snap, like a jaw or something had been broken.

Chase stomped the hand that held Ariel's foot. "Let go, asshole!"

Our movements jarred the debris. A log rolled and soon all the twigs and litter floated downstream. With one more hard kick from Chase, Ariel's foot broke loose. We pulled

Ariel toward the edge of the culvert. A body bobbed up. A woman with long, stringy blonde hair popped out of the water for just a moment. Her jaw, clearly broken, hung slack. Her skin was milk-white, puffy, and tinged blue. We saw her for just a moment, and she reached out toward us, but the water pulled her quickly downstream.

"Oh my God, let's get out of here!" Ariel cried.

Chase, Ariel, and I slogged to the end of the pipe where Puck sat waiting.

"Well, you weren't much help," I told him.

"Your dog drank that water," Chase said, passing me a worried look. "You better keep an eye on him."

I looked at Puck. Was Chase right? What if that woman, that thing, had contaminated the water! I nodded. "Come on, trouble," I told Puck. "At least be some use to us, and lead us back to Vella's truck . . .and don't get sick."

Puck wagged his tail happily, and we headed into the woods. We'd hidden the truck in the thick woods by the field where we'd seen the blue light. From a distance, I could see the corner of the field. I led the others into the woods and headed in that direction. Since Vella and I had come through at night, nothing looked familiar. Puck, however, trotted through the forest like he knew exactly where we were headed, stopping to sniff the ground every few feet. He seemed to be going toward the field, so I followed him. The forest was eerily quiet. The further away we got from the interstate, the safer I felt. We didn't hear any more noise coming from the shopping center; they'd never even known we were nearby. I sighed and looked overhead. Warm rays of light heated the fallen autumn leaves and loamy earth, causing the sweet scent of fall to fill the air. I was taken back to the days when my daddy and I would camp out rather than stay at the carnival bunk houses. We'd find a quiet spot away from the fairgrounds, usually near the trees, and pitch a tent. Lots of times we'd stay up late just roasting marshmallows and telling jokes. You could smell the woods on those nights too, when the campfire would crackle and the dew would come in by dawn.

Trailing behind Puck, it took us half an hour to walk to the edge of the field where Vella and I had hidden her Bronco. It was parked near some small hemlock trees. We had covered the SUV with branches. We stopped before we got too close and hid behind a thicket.

"There," I said to Ariel and Chase as I pointed to the SUV hidden among the trees. "The SUV is hidden just there."

Chase eyed the place over. "Looks clear. I don't see anyone." I heard the worry in his voice. What if Vella and Darius weren't there?

I looked down at Puck. "Go. Go check it out," I told him, pointing to the SUV.

Puck took off in a run, his nose to the ground.

"You see. He is good for something," I whispered to Chase who grinned at me in reply.

Puck sniffed all around the SUV. When he neared the back, almost out of view, he stopped. He lifted his head and gave a muffled, but happy, bark. His tail began to wag.

"Puck?" I heard Vella call.

I sighed with relief. "Vella?" I called. Ariel, Chase, and I came out from behind the thicket and headed toward the SUV.

Vella came around the front of the vehicle and rushed to me, pulling me into a hug. Her body was soaked in sweat, and I could feel her shaking.

"Thank goodness! Those men. . .oh, Cricket!"

"I'm all right. I followed my instincts," I whispered in her ear.

She leaned back, looked at me then nodded affirmatively.

Darius, who had been hiding with Vella, appeared as well. He pulled Chase into a manly hug, clapped him on the back then shook his head.

"What happened down there?" I asked. Both Darius and Vella looked rattled.

"They just appeared out of nowhere, came barreling off the highway. They must have seen the star," Darius said, casting a sad glance at Vella. "Didn't take them long to find the back door. We didn't even have time to warn Elias. We saw eight of them, all armed. Before we could even decide what to do, we heard gunshots. We climbed down the fire escape and ran. I feel sick about it. Did you see anything?"

I nodded. "More came. There were at least a dozen there."

"They shot Gemma," Chase added. "We saw that much and heard worse. . .that baby. . ."

"I don't understand!" Ariel said exasperated. "How can people turn so. . .evil. . .just like that? How can people be normal one week then turn killer a week later? I mean, are people really that screwed up just under the surface? Katy was only five!"

"There are lots of bad people in the world. They walk around looking normal, barely keeping the beast inside them locked up. When there is no law, the beast runs free," Chase said. I couldn't help but notice that his eyes looked haunted. Something told me he had first-hand experience with those kinds of people.

"But those girls!" Ariel shrieked, outraged. "They were just kids!"

I shut my eyes. I didn't want to think about it, but Chase was right. Good people would try to hole up somewhere to survive. Evil people, however, would feel set free. It was always like that. No sooner did a hurricane or tornado pass through a city than people were looting, killing, and God knows what else. So many people, everyday people, were walking around with blackness in their hearts. All they needed was an excuse to set it loose.

"Let's get out of here," I said then.

"Where in the world are we going to go now?" Ariel asked.

I looked at Vella. "We'll follow our instincts," I replied.

Vella nodded knowingly.

"Well, I hope our instincts find us somewhere safe," Darius said gruffly.

"Me too." But where was safe now?

CHAPTER TEN

VELLA PULLED out her tattered old map and spread it across the hood of the Bronco.

"We're here," Ariel said, pointing a chewed fingernail at a spot on the map. All her blue nail polish was gone.

"Where can we go?" Darius asked. "We need somewhere to lay low."

Daruis' words made me feel better. At least I knew for sure we were the *good* people.

"There isn't much out on these state roads, just houses and farms. But Old Towne is on the other side of the valley."

"Old Towne? Wait," I said, looking at the map. "The old Fairway Fun grounds are just outside of Old Towne. You ever do that circuit?" I asked Vella.

She shook her head then started pulling her long, curly black hair into a ponytail. "I was still in Lily Dale back then."

"Lily Dale?" I asked.

"It's a community for mediums in New York State."

Ariel gave Vella a sidelong glance. "You're a medium?"

Vella shrugged. "I read tarot."

"Like. . .for money?"

Vella fixed Ariel with a hard "I dare you to say something" kind of look.

Ariel turned back to the map. "Fairway Fun. . .yeah, I remember the place, I think," Ariel said. "We went to that fair when I was little. I remember the carousel."

I nodded. "They shuttered the place like five years ago. The fairground was surrounded by cow pastures and had a fence topped with razor wire. And," I said excitedly, "there was a brick administration building with an old fallout shelter! I remember my daddy explaining what a fallout shelter was. Might be supplies there. If not, no one else will think of goin' there, and it will be safe." I looked around at everyone. No one seemed sure. I suddenly hoped Vella would say something mystical to confirm if I was right or wrong, but she just stared at the map. "Well?"

"Maybe we should—" Darius began but was cut off by Puck who hopped into the front seat of the Bronco, put his paws on the dashboard, and barked at us.

"The dog says let's go," Chase said with a laugh. "Darius?"

Darius shrugged. "I got nothing anyway. . .probably as good as anywhere. And the shelter should have a radio."

Vella folded up the map. "Let's try to get there before dark."

We all got in. Once more, I got the feeling that Puck, sitting on alert between Vella and me, was leading the way.

RAYS OF SUN made blobs of light on the dirt road ahead of us as we traveled Route 6 toward Old Towne. The sharp scent of fall leaves filled the crisp air. Winter was right around the corner. How in the hell were they going to distribute a vaccine to people before winter? And how would they even find everyone now? Everything had fallen apart. People were scattered to the wind and good people, like Elias, were dying. I clicked on the radio as we drove. The quarantine recordings had stopped. Now there was nothing but static.

"That's encouraging," Darius grumbled.

"We just read this poem in school. . .I don't remember the name, but I remember a couple of lines: *this is the way the world ends; not with a bang but with a whimper,*" Ariel said absently as she looked out the window. "Seems fitting."

"*The Hollow Men,*" Darius said.

"Huh?" Ariel asked.

"The poem. It's called *The Hollow Men* by T. S. Eliot."

Chase shook his head at Darius.

"Is that how you two know each other? Through college?" I asked Chase and Darius. Great, I was the dumbest person in the group.

"Keg State College," Chase said with a laugh. "We were going to a college branch campus. I'd been fixing cars for the last five years, but my mama made me go back, especially when she found out Darius—me and Darius are cousins—was going. I just wanted to work on cars, but because of him, I was sitting in class making no money and learning a bunch of nothing."

I grinned at him.

"What about you?" Ariel asked Darius.

"The church paid my tuition. I wanted to be a math teacher."

"Brian was good at math," Ariel said distractedly.

"What was your major?" I asked Chase.

"Not failing," he replied with a wink. "You go to school?"

I shook my head then lifted my pipe wrench. I was about to tell Chase about the tilt when Vella slowed the Bronco. Down the road ahead, a couple toting heavy backpacks ran from the road into the woods.

"Runnin' scared," I said.

Vella sped up the Bronco again. When we passed the spot along the road where the couple had dodged into the woods, I looked for them. I just caught a glimmer of light reflecting off a backpack. They were hiding in a thicket.

"Not a bad idea," Darius said. "Nothing out there to eat you alive."

"Bears," Vella said.

"I'll take a bear over a zombie any day," he replied.

"Is that what they are? Zombies? Like in the movies?" Ariel asked.

Darius shrugged. "They're sick, that's all. But people are eating people. Cannibals, maybe. But they look . . .like zombies."

Ariel pulled her knees up to her chest then set her head on her knees. A moment later, I heard her crying softly. The sound of it broke my heart. But her sadness was something we all felt. While I still felt like I couldn't wrap my brain around what I was seeing, Ariel was right to be sad. The world was dying. Maybe it didn't hit me as hard because the only person I ever really loved, my daddy, was already dead. Maybe the rest of the world was feeling just like I had when daddy died, like the world had come to an end. I reached back and squeezed Ariel's hand. I knew what it felt like to lose someone you loved. I wouldn't wish it on another soul. But in the end, the whole world was feeling pain just like that. The world was hurting. We had all just lost something big: life as we knew it. I looked out the window. No more tilt-a-whirl, or kids laughing, or cotton candy, or TV re-runs, or new t-shirts, or lipstick, steak dinners at a restaurant—not that I ever had one, but I wanted to—or anything else. Unless somebody found a cure right quick, it was all done.

I then draped my other arm over Puck. He licked my cheek then went back to staring forward like a guard dog. I closed my eyes. That numb feeling started to chip away a bit. I could feel the crack. Maybe I had something to lose after all: life. And I loved life.

—

CHAPTER ELEVEN

WE SLOWED when we reached the intersection of Route 6 and Sungazer Boulevard. The roads were completely empty. There was a hayfield where the driveway leading to the gated fairground used to be; it hadn't been mowed in years. The complex looked deserted. Besides a few farm houses, we hadn't seen any sign of life—living or dead—since the backpackers.

Vella scanned the complex with her binoculars. "Nothing. Nothing moving anywhere."

"Hay is tall," I commented.

"I can't remember the last time they had a fair. I mean, we haven't come here in years," Ariel confirmed.

Vella set her binoculars down and put the Bronco into drive. I looked down the intersecting road. There were no cars anywhere. For a brief moment, I saw a fox run out onto the road. It stopped and looked at us. The engine must have spooked it from the brush. After staring us down, it turned and ran into the woods.

The old fairground driveway, hidden under the tall grass, was bumpy and full of holes. Vella carefully guided the Bronco to the gate. My gun reloaded and ready, I sat waiting for anything.

There was a clang-clang-clang sound when we arrived at the gate. Puck jumped out the window and ran to investigate. An old metal sign was hung over the top of the gate: *Closed for the Season.* The sign was rusty. One corner had broken free, and it dangled loosely, clattering against the gate.

We all got out and went to investigate.

Vella handed me a crowbar. I jammed it under the lock and pulled. The lock popped. I grabbed the rusted metal chain and pulled it off, dropping it to the ground. My hands were covered in rust. I wiped them on my jeans leaving long streaks of orange rust. Great.

Darius and Chase pushed the gates open. They screeched in protest. Vella drove the Bronco just inside, parking it near the gate.

"I'll leave it here in case we need it fast," she said.

Chase and Darius closed the gate behind us. Ariel grabbed a yellow bungee cord that had been lying in the back of the Bronco and started weaving it around the busted lock. Chase pulled the cord tight, but it still didn't seem like enough.

"We need to find some chain," Darius said, echoing my thoughts.

I nodded. "The swings. If the swings are still here we'll have plenty of chain."

"Let's go look," Vella said, and we headed inside.

The place was eerily quiet. The booths were all closed up, their paint chipped off from the weather. We passed the bumper cars pavilion. The cars had been covered by a blue tarp that had torn loose. The little cars looked rusted. No doubt they'd sat under snow for more than one winter.

"Where is the fallout shelter?" Vella asked, scanning around.

"There," I pointed to a large concrete block building a few aisles over.

"Let's make sure we don't already have company," Chase suggested.

We headed in the direction of the cornflower blue building. Its paint was worn off, but I could see that all around the top of the building someone had painted the words: *Giggle, Cheer, Delight. . .You're at Fairway Fun Tonight.* I really hoped so. Not only was the massive building abandoned, but what window it did have at the front—from which they used to sell corndogs—was bolted down with a metal hurricane shutter. Darius tried the door: locked. The faded blue and orange fallout shelter sign was still attached to the wall by the door. At least we were in the right place.

Chase investigated the lock. "You got a toolkit in your SUV?" he asked Vella.

"Yes. Not much to it, but I've got the basics."

"I can get the lock. I'll need some tools and a little minute, but I'll have it open in no time."

"It's getting late," Ariel commented as she looked skeptically at the sky. The late afternoon sun was already beginning to dim.

"Let's split up," I suggested. "You and Vella grab the

tools, and we'll get the chain, lock the gate down, and check the other entrances."

With a nod, we headed off in different directions.

"This way," I said, eyeing the buildings. I could just see the top of the swings. It felt weird being back at Fairway Fun. With my heart thundering in my chest, expecting to get jumped by a zombie any minute, it was hard to think of anything else but getting inside that building and being safe. Around every turn, however, I remembered the last time I was there with my daddy.

We passed the Ladies Auxiliary booth. "They used to have great steak sandwiches," I said wistfully, calling up memories of me and my daddy sitting at the red picnic tables nearby, eating steak sandwiches and brushing away wasps who'd come looking for a sip of lemonade.

"So you worked at the carnival?" Ariel asked. I could see from the look in her eyes that she was both interested and a little disgusted. Townies always treated us like that. I'd gotten used to it.

"I'm a tilt girl," I told her, feeling the pride swell in my chest. After all, there was no higher honor in carnie life than being a ride operator. Everyone knew that.

"A tilt girl?" Darius asked.

I nodded. "I had a tilt-a-whirl. . .well, me and my daddy before he died, then just me. I ran the tilt."

Ariel giggled. "Those are so much fun," she said with a bright smile. I knew that smile. It was the kind of smile only a tilt could produce. I wanted to crush Ariel in my arms and hug the life out of her for smiling like that.

"What about you, Darius? You like rides? Coasters?"

Darius shook his head. "Makes me puke," he said with a laugh.

I grinned at him. I think that was the first time he'd smiled since I met him. Leave it to the carnival to bring out the laughter in people.

When we got to the swings, we were happy to find that someone had already taken down the seats and stowed them in an unlocked container. We were able to unhook as much chain as we could carry. Since the chains had been locked up, they weren't rusty, but the metal was still sharp. I cursed under my breath as the rough steel cut my fingers. Finally, we headed back to the gate. Vella and Chase were already gone. I hoped they were having as much luck as we were. We locked up the front gate then headed around the perimeter.

"I think there are two more gates," I said as we pushed through the tall grass.

"Watch for any holes in the fence," Darius called.

We chained up the second gate and headed toward the back of the park to the crew and farm entrance. Along the way, we passed behind the big 4H sheds. Even though the animals were gone, the lingering scent of horse manure and chicken shit wafted from the place. I always hated the farm show sections of the carnival. They smelled rancid, but were still a great place to troll for cowboys or farmers' sons. I'd come to learn that the bigger their belt buckle was, the bigger their—

"Look," Ariel said, snapping me from my thoughts.

We'd reached the back gate. It was wide open. "That's not good."

We glanced around. The place was still dead silent. We didn't even hear Chase and Vella. I studied the ground. The road was overgrown and undisturbed. There were no tire tracks or footprints. I did, however, spot some animal prints in the dust. They were small and cat-like. They looked like they may have belonged to a fox. Foxes must have been common in this neck of the woods.

Puck put his nose to the ground and started sniffing. When he hit on the fox tracks, he growled low and dangerous. His ears flattened, and the hackles on his back rose.

"It's just a fox, Puck. It's people we need to watch out for," I told him.

Puck, ignoring me as usual, kept his nose to the ground and ran off, following the fox tracks. I was glad he was going to be fenced in with the rest of us. I'd about had it risking my neck for that dog.

"It looks clear," I said then swung the gate shut. Carefully, Darius, Ariel, and I closed and chained up the gate. We swept the fence one more time just to be sure it was clear. Everything seemed in order. If anyone or anything was trying to get in, they would have to make a hell of a lot of noise to do it. And the razor wire running around the top of the gate was surely a deterrent. With the rest of the fence clear of breaches, we felt safe. In our own little fortress, we were protected from everything except the occasional fox.

CHAPTER TWELVE

WE HEADED BACK to the administrative building. It was strange how quiet it was. It was like all the noise in the world had switched off. There were no planes in the sky. There was no rev of engines. It was just . . .quiet. All you could hear was the wind whistling down the aisles. When we got to the admin building, we found the door wide open.

Darius looked at me and raised an eyebrow.

"Vella?" I called from the doorway.

No answer.

Darius and I pulled our guns, and the three of us entered carefully. The place had a sharp, musty smell. Inside was a small kitchenette where they used to make the corndogs. An empty hot pretzel machine, soda fountain, and several moldy bottles of ketchup sat on the counter facing the dusty tables inside. Once we were inside, we saw that Chase and Vella had opened an interior door that led downstairs.

"Vella!" I called again.

After a few minutes, I heard a screech followed by the sound of footsteps on the stairs. Vella appeared. "You won't believe this. Come take a look!" she said excitedly.

We followed her back downstairs. The basement itself was dank, but on the far side of the cavernous space was another open door. From inside, light shined out. Then I heard the crackling sound of radio: "The United States and Canada are no-fly zones. All major US cities are now under quarantine. Citizens are advised to stay in their homes. International aid is delayed. Reports of the contaminant reaching Europe and Asia are confirmed. Government officials have been moved to a secure location. Avoid direct contact with the diseased. Origin of the contaminant still unknown. Looping Radio. Office of Civil Defense Fallouts. Standby . . ." the recording buzzed then began again. Chase turned it down.

I gazed around at the fallout shelter. The walls and ceiling were made of some kind of heavy metal. The floor was poured concrete which had been painted white. The shelter was constructed as two rooms. In the first room, the walls were lined with a dozen cots. The radio stand sat just behind them. Chase sat turning the dials.

"This is the only station coming in. For the moment, we have electricity, but there is a generator here. No gas though."

"Great," Darius said with a frown.

"What is this place?" Ariel asked.

"Fallout shelter from the 1950s," Darius replied. "They

built a ton of these during the Cold War. Everyone thought the Russians were going to start a war."

"The Russians? Why?"

"Because the Russians are crazy," Vella spat.

I headed toward the back room. There, the walls were lined with row after row of boxes marked *Survival Supplies: Furnished by the Office of Civil Defense.* One box was opened. A tarnished metal can with the words *Survival Crackers* written on the side was sitting on the shelf. And the expiration date? 1972.

"Well, these would kill us," I said, lifting the box. "We need to scavenge around the grab joints. There has to be some somethin' left behind. We passed the Boy Scouts' place just down the aisle. We can start there."

"We need to find water," Ariel said. "We can last without food for a couple of days, but we need water."

"Should be some faucets around. Let's go look before it gets dark. Besides, that goddamned dog of mine ran off again. Need to round him up before we lock in for the night."

"That dog is going get you killed," Chase said.

I had to chuckle. Chase was right. Puck was becoming a nuisance, but that was partially why I loved him. He was just as mischievous as me. "What can I do? He's my only love."

Chase grinned slickly at me. "Someone needs to change that, before you end up dead."

"What, you gonna try to romance me?" I certainly hoped so.

"Only to save your life," he said with a smirk.

"Well, aren't you a gentleman."

Darius chuckled. "Come on," he said, and we all headed back upstairs.

IT WAS ALREADY dusk by the time we started canvasing the fairgrounds. Chase, Ariel, and I headed in one direction; Darius and Vella went the other. The first two food stalls we checked were empty. And while the electricity was still on, the water had been turned off.

"No luck," I said as I turned a faucet on a pipe beside one of the grab joints.

"Need to look for bottled water then," Ariel said.

"The Ladies Auxiliary stall was this way," I said, leading them down the aisle toward the food stand.

The grab joint was locked up, but I had brought my wrench. With a heave, I busted open the lock. The sound of the metal blasting apart the lock and wood echoed. We all stilled.

"Scary," Ariel said. "It's so quiet."

"As a sinner at Sunday mass," I agreed, pushing open the door. She was right; the silence was unnerving.

The stall smelled like it had been boarded up for a couple of years, but it was arranged neatly. And inside, we finally had some luck.

"Anyone in the mood for tomatoes?" Chase asked, lifting a two-gallon can of crushed tomatoes. He turned it to examine the label. "Still good!"

I sighed. This was never going to work. We might be

good here for a couple of days, but we were going to have to find more supplies very soon.

"Here," Ariel said, pulling a plastic milk crate from off the top of the fridge. "Let's fill this." She and Chase started filling up the basket with cans of tomatoes.

I started opening the drawers. There wasn't much else except packets of salt and pepper which I stuffed into my jeans pocket. As I stuffed my hand in my jeans, I realized how filthy I felt. I hadn't changed my clothes in a couple of days. I could feel the gooey velvet of plaque on my teeth, and my armpits smelled none too pretty. Of course, everyone else looked and smelled like I did. But still, I felt gross.

I gazed out the window of the stall. Across from me was the carousel. It made me sad to see it left open to the weather like that. Of course, the animals were plastic, not painted wood like some of the real nice old carousels. But the paint, even on the plastic, had started to fade. I scanned over the menagerie of creatures: horses, dragons, zebras, over-grown fish, unicorns, lions. Then, I saw movement. For a split second, I thought I saw someone standing among the animals. My stomach dropped to the pit of my stomach.

When I turned, Ariel and Chase were still working. "Look Cricket," Ariel said, "they must have sold chili," she added, holding up two big cans of beans.

I nodded mutely. "Yeah, be sure to grab a pot. And look for some matches. We'll need to start a campfire." I cast a glance back outside. The window was really dirty, and the glass had a bevel in it that made the outside image wavy-looking. I gazed back at the carousel. I swore I could still see someone there.

Wordlessly, I stepped around Chase and Ariel. "Feels tight in here. I'll be just outside," I said then stepped out of the stall.

"Stay close," Chase said. "And don't go after that dog. He'll come back, especially once he smells food."

"Yeah, yeah," I called back. I pulled my weapon from the back of my jeans and firmed up my grip on my wrench. Carefully, I went toward the carousel. From my view at the window, I would have bet my life that someone had been standing near the lion. I raised my gun and moved slowly toward the carousel. I eyed the carousel menagerie animals, scanning for the lion. The sunflower-yellow paint on his plastic fur had faded. The lion's lips looked too red. I stilled when I saw movement on the other side of the carousel. Someone or something was moving away from me, going deeper into the park. A pair of mourning doves in the aisle on the other side of the ride spooked. Cooing in alarm, they fluttered to the roof of a grab joint nearby.

Keeping my gun in front of me, I moved carefully onto the carousel. I grabbed the metal pole attached to a faded green dragon and started to move around the edge of the ride to the other side. The animal's open mouths had always seemed so fun and playful. Now they grinned grotesquely, their black eyes bulging, their red lips looking bloody. My heart slammed in my chest. On the other side of the ride was a row of game booths. There, I saw the shadow of a man reflected on the wall of a one of the booths. The shadow didn't move; it just stood there.

Slowly, I stepped off the carousel. Gun raised, I approached the shadowy figure. "Who are you?" I called. "Step out."

The figure didn't move.

Beads of sweat trickled from my brow down my cheek. I could feel the sweat dripping from my chin. My heart was beating so loud I could hear it thundering in my ears.

Moving slowly, I entered the space between the buildings. Whoever they were, they weren't moving. I remembered how Beau had just stood there in the mist when Vella and I ran into him. My hands shook; I held my gun tightly. I took a deep breath then stepped into view of the figure casting the shadow, my finger ready to pull the trigger.

Then, I saw it. In front of the game booth was a wooden silhouette of a magician. The game booth had been used by people who could do slight-of-hand tricks, real rabbit-out-of-the-hat kind of shows. The magician was cut so he was holding his hat in his hands, a cute white bunny looking out. The paint was faded, but he had been painted with a handle-bar moustache that curled at the corners, and he wore a pin-striped suit. He reminded me of the bad guy from the *Frosty the Snowman* movie.

"You almost gave me a damned heart attack," I told the magician. Then I heard a loud clatter like someone had overturned a toolbox. I looked across the aisle. I lowered my gun. To my great surprise, across the aisle was a tilt-a-whirl. And lo and behold, Puck was sitting beside the ticket stand.

"Well, found your way home, did you?" I asked with a laugh. I snapped the safety back on my gun and stuck it back into the back of my jeans. Puck whined happily and wagged his tail just a little, but then he stood and circled around nervously, watching in every direction.

"What is it, baby?" I asked, bending to pet him. He was shaking. It wasn't like Puck to be so unnerved.

"Don't let that old fool scare you," I said, waving a hand toward the magician. "He's nothing but wood. I damned near shot him," I added with a laugh then rose to look at the tilt. She was broken down, that was for sure. Someone must have towed her in and left her there to rust. She wasn't even fully set up. The seats were still pushed together, her red and blue paint faded. My daddy would have loved a find like this. What a challenge!

"Tomorrow, we'll check her out," I told Puck.

Puck only whimpered in reply and looked around nervously, casting glances up and down the aisle.

"Geez, Puck, you're giving me the willies," I told him. Puck never got spooked. Maybe he'd just seen too much the last few days.

"Cricket?" I heard Chase call. "Girl, where did you go now?"

"Cricket?" Ariel echoed after him.

"Come on, let's go," I told Puck. I took one last look around then headed back across the carousel platform to Chase and Ariel, who stood waiting with three milk crates full of food and supplies.

"Hey, you found him!" Ariel said with a smile, patting Puck's head.

I nodded but didn't say much else. I didn't want them

worried over nothing. After all, it had just been my mind playing trick on me.

"I'll grab that one," I said, bending to pick up a crate.

Chase and Ariel started back toward the fallout shelter, Puck padding along behind them. When I stood up, I looked back at the carousel. And for a brief moment, I saw the reflection of a tall, red-haired woman in the carousel's mirrors. I tilted my head to get a better look, but the image shifted and was gone.

"Coming, Cricket?" Ariel called.

"Yeah," I called weakly then followed after them. *Got a screw loose,* my daddy would have said. *Be careful, you're acting like you got a screw loose.* The shadows were just playing tricks on me. No doubt some fallout shelter chili would fix me right up.

CHAPTER THIRTEEN

"NOTHING ELSE. . .just that same recording over and over again," Darius said as he dialed through the radio channels for what seemed like the five-hundredth time. He jammed his plastic spoon back into his Styrofoam cup full of luke-warm, spice-free chili then leaned back in his chair.

After cooking up a quick pot of chili at a small campfire just outside the administrative building, we had locked up the place and battened down the hatches of the fallout shelter for the night. Despite feeling really claustrophobic, the place also felt very safe.

I sat down on the cot beside Vella and was about to tell her about the tilt-a-whirl that Puck had found when I saw she was totally engrossed with her cards. Her brow was furrowed as she shuffled them over and over again. She would stop, pull one card, frown, then stick it back in the deck and shuffle again. This time, however, when she pulled out a card, I took it gently from her.

"Judgment?" I eyed the image on the card. Angelic

looking creatures raised their hands to the sky in prayer just as a wave was about to wash over them.

"Reversed," Vella clarified, as if it meant something important. If so, I didn't know what.

"You keep gettin' the same card?" I asked her.

She nodded.

"What does it mean?"

Vella puckered her lips then arched her thick black eyebrows, her forehead furrowing with worry as she shook her head.

"Let me try," Chase said, sitting across from us.

I handed the card back to Vella, and she reshuffled. "Cut the deck then show the bottom card," she told Chase.

He did what he was told. I tried not to gasp out loud when he turned over the Judgment card.

"So, what *does* it mean?" Chase asked Vella.

"The waters are rising," Vella said, her voice shaking. "We better get some rest." She stuffed her tarot cards back into her bag.

Ariel, Chase, and Vella crawled into their cots and slept. Darius sat playing with the radio. Again and again it played the quarantine alert. Puck crawled onto the foot of my cot, but he didn't sleep. He kept lifting his head at every little sound. I stared at the cot above me and tried not to think about shadows, or rising water, or anything else.

I WAS the first one to wake up the next morning thanks to Puck, who had started dancing in front of the door fifteen minutes earlier. I could tell from his whine that he really needed to go.

"Okay," I whispered quietly. "Don't wake everyone up. I'm comin'," I told him as I rose groggily. I pulled on my boots then opened the door as quietly as I could. Just like a bank vault door, the fallout shelter door had a metal wheel. I turned the wheel hard: I could hear it unbarring the pins between the frame and the bunker wall. After a moment, the door opened with a squeak. To my surprise, no one else woke. It was no wonder. We were all exhausted.

Puck wiggled out the door and headed upstairs. Still wiping the sleep from my eyes, I followed him. "I'm comin'," I groaned tiredly. But when I got to the top of the stairs, I was surprised to see Puck standing there with his teeth bared. He growled low then crouched, his hackles rising.

The sound had been dampened by the fallout shelter; we never heard them. I could see their shadows under the door and around the shuttered window. They pounded on the door, pushed on the window covering. There was no mistaking their groan. The zombies had come. We were totally surrounded.

CHAPTER FOURTEEN

"WHAT IS ALL THAT NOISE?" Darius asked sleepily as he climbed the stairs.

"Shhh!" I hissed at him.

When he reached the top of the stairs, Darius' eyes went wide. "Where did they come from?" he mouthed to me.

I shook my head.

My heart was thundering in my chest. Darius pointed back downstairs. We rushed back down. Puck bolted ahead of us. When we reached the shelter, Darius swung the door closed, trying to be as quiet as possible, and locked the door.

"Wake up," Darius told Chase, shaking Chase's shoulder.

"Man, come on," Chase complained.

"Ariel, Vella, wake up. We're in trouble," I whispered to them.

"Get up. We're surrounded," Darius told Chase.

"Surrounded by what?" Ariel asked as she started pulling on her sneakers.

"Those sick people. . .those zombies," I told her. "They're practically busting down the door up there."

"How? We locked the whole place up!" Ariel exclaimed.

"Doesn't matter," Vella answered. "The flood is here. Don't curse the tide, run from it."

"Shouldn't we stay here? We're safe in here, right?" Ariel said.

"Safe, yes, but we'll starve to death if they don't wander off. And for whatever reason, they know we are in here." I replied.

"Grab everything," Chase said, and we started filling our bags.

Darius flung open the supply cupboard and pulled out a crowbar and a shovel. He held them out to Ariel. "Pick your poison." She took the shovel.

"There is a back door upstairs," Vella said.

"Go quiet and stick together," I told everyone as I opened the shelter door. "And you, stay with us!" I scolded Puck.

Carefully, we opened the door. From above, we could hear the zombies banging on the door. They hadn't broken through yet. We moved slowly up the stairs. When we got to main room, we could still see their shadows and hear their groans. There were at least a dozen of them trying to get in.

"Back door," Darius whispered.

Vella led us to the musty smelling storage room in the

back. Tables and chairs filled the space. No one was banging on the metal back door. We all stilled and listened.

"There," Ariel said, pointing to the window above the door. "Boost me up," she told Darius. "I'll look out."

Darius locked his fingers. Balancing herself, holding onto his shoulders, Ariel pulled herself up. Darius backed against the door so Ariel could steady herself. I saw him turn his face away from her body as her bare stomach and the front of her jeans brushed his face. In spite of himself, he smiled.

Ariel's fingers gripped the top of the door frame: she looked out. "I don't see anyone."

Carefully, Darius lowered her back down. A smile passed between them when they were face to face, him holding her by the waist. Well, if we didn't die in the next five minutes, I supposed that could turn into something.

Vella and I looked at one another. We were running again. I was very glad she was with me.

"We'll head back to the Bronco. Quick and quiet," I whispered.

Everyone nodded. Slowly, Chase unlocked the door. It opened with a click. Giving it a little shove with his shoulder, he popped the door open. From the other side of the building, we head loud groans.

"Let's go," Vella said, and we took off, running from the flood.

CHAPTER FIFTEEN

IT DIDN'T TAKE us long to figure out that while we had outsmarted the zombies banging down our front door, they were the least of our worries. The place was creeping with sick people. It looked like all of Old Towne had come for the fair. No sooner had we turned down one aisle than we ran into a hulking man. He wore a faded Aerosmith t-shirt and no pants. He was just roaming the world in his tighty-whities, white froth dripping from his mouth. His moon-white eyes centered on Vella. He lunged at her.

Before she could move, Darius dropped a crowbar on his head. The first blow slowed him down but it wasn't until the third strike that he finally dropped.

"They're everywhere!" Ariel shrieked. "What the hell!" Already some of the others, hearing the commotion, turned toward us.

"This way," I said. "We'll head through the rides, cross the bumper cars."

We hustled down the aisle, running as fast as we could.

When I looked back, I could see a horde chasing us. We passed the pony ride corrals and headed toward the games. We had just turned the corner at the duck pond when a group of five more came at us. Among them were two small children.

The children were fast. They gritted their teeth and sprinted at us.

Vella swung, taking out the first one with the high striker mallet. Chase aimed his gun at the second, but she moved too fast. In a split second, she lunged at Ariel, knocking her to the ground. The shovel tumbled from Ariel's hand.

Puck barked and grabbed the child by the pant leg, pulling her away from Ariel who kicked and wiggled as the girl snapped at her. I pulled out my big hunting knife. Chase kicked the girl off, and I quickly dropped the knife on her head. The unholy light faded from her dim eyes. I saw that my cut had also severed her braid. Her yellow hair slipped to the ground, its pretty unicorn bow still attached. My heart broke, but I didn't have a chance to think on it because a second later, I heard a gunshot. I turned to see Chase shooting at the others advancing on us. I cringed. The gunshots would draw the others in. Chase dropped the woman advancing on him while Darius smashed an elderly man in the head. But no sooner were they down then the horde that had been chasing us, plus several more, caught up.

"Run!" Chase yelled.

Darius helped Ariel up, and we all took off. I was at the back of the group, Puck running beside me. When I looked back, I saw that there were now more than twenty of them after us. We ran down a side row toward the rides. I was following the others when a group of zombies pushed open the door of a game stall between me and the rest of the group, cutting me off.

"Cricket!" Vella yelled.

I stopped dead in my tracks and backed up. "Go! Go! Don't stop! I'm coming," I called. I turned and fled around the back of the long building. The horde that had been in the building pursued me.

"Cricket! Hurry!" I heard Ariel yell. I could tell from the sound of her voice that they were running in the opposite direction.

Moments later I found myself in front of the Ladies Axillary joint. I cast a glance behind me. They were gaining on me, and there were more of them now. I needed to cut across the aisle to catch up to Vella and the others. I ran to the carousel and started picking my way to the other side. The carousel platform shook when three zombies jumped onto the ride with me. They were so fast. Why were they so fast?

Puck turned and barked at them, growling and baring his teeth. He grabbed the pant leg of one of the zombies and tugged him hard. The man stumbled then fell against the game controls. A second later, the carousel lights flickered on and, moving very slowly, the carousel started to spin. The sweet, tinkling sound of carousel music chimed. One of the zombies teetered then fell into the horns of a carousel bull. The bull impaled him in the gut. He was stuck. The zombie struggled to get free.

The ride, which had sat idle for years, was unstable. The platform jerked, knocking me off balance, banging me between an overgrown eagle and a prancing horse. I grabbed the plastic horse's bridle to steady myself, but the fake leather bridle snapped in my hand. I fell. It was a weird sensation. I hit my head hard on the metal platform. Pain seared across my skull. I felt like my eyes were going to bulge out of their sockets. Dark spots flitted in front of my eyes and for a second, my eyes closed. I slid across the platform. Barely aware, I grabbed the footrest of a nearby lion and held on. I looked at the mirrors overhead. I saw paintings of cherubs carrying wreaths and playing trumpets as they flew across the sky behind a dancing girl who swung a parade master's baton. My eyes fluttered open and closed. I wanted to sleep. I forced my eyes open just a crack to see a zombie approaching me. Puck put himself between us. He lunged. The zombie fell off the ride. As the carousel spun, the zombie who had fallen into the ride gears pushed himself up. When he did so, he pushed the acceleration gear. The carousel began to spin quickly. The colored lights flickered on and off. The carousel music continued to chime. At least a dozen more zombies got on the ride. I saw their bloody clothes, froth dripping in long strings from their mouths, as they moved toward me. Puck whimpered nervously. I could barely keep my eyes open. My head ached. I looked across the aisle to see the tilt-a-whirl. If I could get off the carousel, maybe I could make it to the tilt. I couldn't think of a better place to die.

I tried to crawl to the edge of the carousel, but my head felt like it was splitting open. All I wanted to do was sleep.

Again and again, the carousel spun past the tilt-a-whirl. It felt like a sick joke. Puck nosed me under my chin, trying to rouse me then whimpered. Through my cloudy eyes I saw that the first zombie had finally reached me. I also realized that the back of my head felt wet. Was I bleeding? Wiggling, I pulled the gun out of the back of my jeans, but my fingers were weak. I dropped the weapon. Puck barked loudly at the zombie then looked at me. He whimpered. I closed my eyes. *I'll be with you soon, Daddy.*

I felt the zombie grab my boot with a jerking wrench. I couldn't open my eyes. My heart slammed in my chest. Maybe I would just die of a heart attack. Puck made a weird half-grunt, half-bark sound then yelped as if in pain.

"Puck," I moaned softly. They had killed him.

Seconds later, I heard a gunshot, then another, then another. Then someone picked me up.

"Not here," a man's voice said. "Of all places, not here."

With the last of my strength, I opened my eyes just a crack. A tall and very attractive young man with long, dark hair and gold-colored eyes was looking down at me as he rushed me away from the carousel. . .and the zombies.

"Hold on, Crick," he said as my eyes fluttered closed again. "I've got you."

CHAPTER SIXTEEN

"IS SHE ALIVE?" I heard Vella ask.

"She is. I found her on the carousel. She was passed out, but she's coming around now," the man replied.

"Come on, come on," Ariel yelled in a panic. "They're coming!"

I heard gunshots.

I opened my eyes just a bit to see I was lying in the back of the Bronco. I heard the screech of the fairground gate opening. The engine turned on.

"We're good," Darius said as he jumped into the front seat.

"Chase, get in," Darius yelled. "Let's go!"

I tried to sit up. What was happening? I wanted to see.

"Easy," the golden-eyed man as he gently helped me sit up. "Your head is bleeding," he added. I realized then that he was holding a rag against the back of my head.

Ariel, and then Chase, climbed into the back of the Bronco, slamming the tailgate closed behind them.

"Where's Puck?" Ariel asked.

The man shook his head. "The dog. . . he's gone."

I closed my eyes. Hot tears stream down my face. "He tried to save me," I whispered. My head hurt. I had no idea how we'd outrun the horde chasing me, but we had. . .and I had Puck to thank for it. I wiped my tears then opened my eyes just a little and looked out the back window of the Bronco. What looked like a hundred zombies chased us.

"Thank God you were there, man," Chase told the stranger.

"I scaled the fence this morning. I was looking for a quiet place to get some rest."

I realized then that the stranger had some sort of accent. It wasn't southern or Irish or anything I'd ever heard before. It was just. . .different. I wiped the tears from my cheeks. "Who do I thank for savin' my life?"

The stranger smiled at me. "Tristan."

"Thank you, Tristan."

"My pleasure," he said then wiped a tear off my cheek. To my surprise, the gesture felt okay.

"Someone tell me where to go," Vella yelled from the front as she drove away from the fairground.

Ariel, who I noticed then was covered in blood and had a big gash on her forehead, pulled out the map. "I don't know! There is nothing around here. We're rural. Just small towns and lots of farms. Maybe we need to find a house. Lay low."

"That hasn't worked out so well so far," Chase said.

"I still don't understand. How the hell did they get in?"

Ariel exclaimed. "Were the gates open? Did you see anything?" she asked, turning to Tristan.

"I saw animal tracks, that is certain, but no living people."

I closed my eyes and pressed the palms of my hands into my eye sockets. Puck was gone. Puck was dead. But at least he had died at the fair, by the tilt-a-whirl. At least he had died somewhere that felt like home.

"Turn left at the junction," Tristan said then, surprising us.

Vella looked back at Tristan. "Left? Why?" Her eyes narrowed as she studied him, but after a moment, I saw her dark eyes widen.

"Left to where?" Darius asked. There was a hard edge on his voice.

"Where I was going. There is an old place. . .about fifty miles from here. It's a very old building. Very high walls. Remote. It will be. . .safe."

"What kind of building. Like a castle or something?" Ariel asked.

"Something like that," Tristan answered. He held Vella's gaze. "All right with you, Vella?"

Vella and Tristan gave one another a long, hard look.

"It will be safe," he told her softly.

I wondered why the rest of us were being left out of the conversation. There was something to be read between the lines, I just didn't know what.

I glanced at Chase. He looked perplexed.

"So, left?" Vella asked Tristan, her gaze softening.

"There is nowhere else in the world to go," he replied with a grin.

Vella smiled, shook her head, and then turned left. As we drove away from the fairground, I watched the zombies rush after us. It was a disgusting sight: humans chasing humans, blood and milky saliva dripping from their mouths, crazed moon-white eyes. For a brief moment, however, I spotted a fox sitting at the edge of the road. It turned and disappeared into the grass. I closed my eyes and took a deep breath. The world had died, but by dumb luck, I had stayed alive. I hoped to keep it that way. I looked up at Tristan who smiled softly at me. From a distance, I heard the soft notes of the carousel music carry on the wind.

Ready to see how Cricket and Layla join forces?

The Complete Harvesting Series Now Available

The Harvesting

Midway

The Shadow Aspect

Witch Wood

The Torn World

ABOUT THE AUTHOR

New York Times and *USA Today* bestselling author Melanie Karsak is the author of *The Road to Valhalla Series, The Celtic Blood Series, Steampunk Red Riding Hood,* and *Steampunk Fairy Tales.* The author currently lives in Florida with her husband and two children.

KEEP IN TOUCH WITH THE AUTHOR ONLINE

facebook.com/melaniekarsak
twitter.com/melaniekarsak
instagram.com/karsakmelanie
pinterest.com/melaniekarsak
bookbub.com/authors/melanie-karsak

ALSO BY MELANIE KARSAK

The Celtic Blood Series:

Highland Raven

Highland Blood

Highland Vengeance

Highland Queen

The Road to Valhalla Series:

Under the Blood Moon

Shield-Maiden: Under the Howling Moon

Shield-Maiden: Under the Hunter's Moon

Shield-Maiden: Under the Thunder Moon

Shield-Maiden: Under the Blood Moon

Shield-Maiden: Under the Dark Moon

Steampunk Fairy Tales:

Curiouser and Curiouser: Steampunk Alice in Wonderland

Ice and Embers: Steampunk Snow Queen

Beauty and Beastly: Steampunk Beauty and the Beast

Golden Braids and Dragon Blades: Steampunk Rapunzel

Steampunk Red Riding Hood:

Wolves and Daggers

Alphas and Airships

Peppermint and Pentacles

Bitches and Brawlers

Howls and Hallows

Lycans and Legends

Steampunk Christmas Fairy Tales

Goblins and Snowflakes: An Elves and the Shoemaker Retelling

Hauntings and Humbug: A Christmas Carol Retelling

Frostbitten Fairy Tales: A Christmas Fairy Tale Collection (available seasonally)

The Airship Racing Chronicles:

Chasing the Star Garden

Chasing the Green Fairy

Chasing Christmas Past

The Chancellor Fairy Tales:

The Glass Mermaid

The Cupcake Witch

The Fairy Godfather

Made in United States
North Haven, CT
20 April 2023

35685423R00071